Feeling Sor

Jaclyn Moriarty grew up in Sydney, Australia, with four sisters, one brother, two dogs and twelve chickens. She studied English and Law at the University of Sydney, and then spent a year in the US doing a Masters at Yale, and a further three years in England, writing a PhD at Cambridge. When she returned home, the chickens had blown away in a thunderstorm.

She now lives in Sydncy with a handsome Canadian, and works as a media and entertainment lawyer. Her favourite things to do at weekends are sleeping in, going to the beach and eating popcorn at the cinema.

Feeling Sorry For Celia

Jaclyn Moriarty

MACMILLAN CHILDREN'S BOOKS

First published 2000 by Pan Macmillan Publishers Australia

First published in the UK 2001 by Macmillan Children's Books
a division of Macmillan Publishers Limited
25 Eccleston Place, London SW1W 9NF
Basingstoke and Oxford
www.macmillan.com

Associated companies throughout the world

ISBN 0 330 39725 7

A CIP catalogue record for this book is available from
the British Library.

Phototypeset by Intype London Ltd
Printed and bound in Great Britain by Mackays of Chatham plc, Kent

To my family,
including Grandma,
and to Colin

Acknowledgements

I am very grateful to the following people for their invaluable assistance with this book: my agents Garth Nix, Jonathan Lloyd and Jill Grinberg, and my editors Marion Lloyd, Anna McFarlane and Alicia Brooks. I am also grateful to Rachel Amamoo, Michael Sobkin, and Alice Woolley, and would especially like to thank Corrie Stepan.

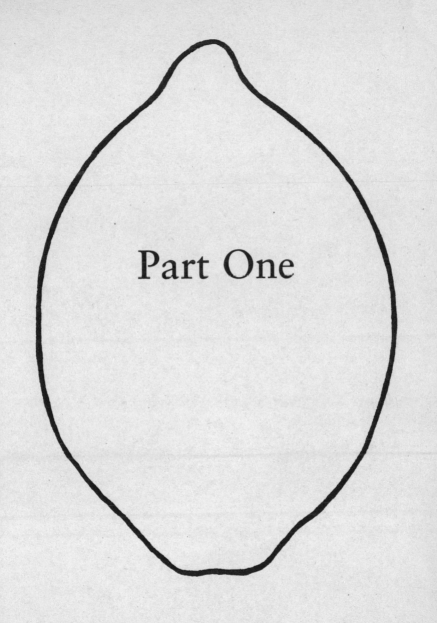

Part One

Dear Ms Clarry,

It has come to our attention that you are incredibly bad at being a teenager.

I mean, take a look at your bedroom.

You haven't got any posters on your wall. (Don't try to tell us that that picture counts. A kitten drowning in a strawberry milkshake? Designed by your mother as an ad for carpet cleaner? Give us a break.)

You have a paper chain made of old Christmas cards hanging from your curtain rail. The only make-up you have is banana flavoured lip gloss and it's melting all over your Little Mermaid quilt cover. (Actually, we don't think that lip gloss counts as make-up at all.)

Not to hurt your feelings or anything, but you are an embarrassment to teenagerhood. Therefore, could you please climb into the refrigerator and wait very quietly until your teenage years end?

Thank you.

Yours sincerely,
The Association of Teenagers

P.S. Also, you don't seem to understand how to get a snow tan. You look like a slice of watermelon.

!!!!! IMPORTANT !!!!! LOOK AT THIS NOTE !!!!
!!! ELIZABETH !!!!! OVER HERE !!!! ON THE FRIDGE !!!!!

LIBBY,

I HOPE YOU SAW THIS NOTE.
   GOOD MORNING.
   EAT THE PORRIDGE IN <u>THE BIG SILVER SAUCEPAN</u>
<u>ON THE STOVE.</u> PUT SOME ALOE ON YOUR FACE.
<u>DON'T BURN YOUR FACE LIKE THAT AGAIN. YOUR</u>
<u>SKIN WILL ALL PEEL AWAY AND THERE WILL BE</u>
<u>NOTHING LEFT BUT BONES AND BRAIN AND EYEBALLS.</u>
   IT IS <u>VERY AND EXTREMELY</u> COLD TODAY. WEAR
SEVEN PAIRS OF STOCKINGS.
   HAVE A NICE FIRST DAY BACK AT SCHOOL.

                         LOVE FROM YOUR THOUGHTFUL AND
                              CONSIDERATE MOTHER

Mum,

Take it easy. I saw the note.

I didn't eat the porridge, I gave it to Lochie. I hate porridge. If you really cared about me, you would know that.

I am not wearing any stockings at all. It's not that cold. You have some kind of body temperature problem.

The really weird thing is that I didn't burn my face like this on purpose.

And I'm not using aloe because it's disgusting.

4

Thank you for your nice warning about the bones and brains and eyeballs though.

> With lots of love
> from your daughter Elizabeth

Dear Ms Clarry,

It is with great pleasure that we invite you to join our Society.

We have just found out about your holiday. It's so impressive! You had four assignments, an English essay and a chapter of Maths to do. And you didn't do one single piece of homework!

Fabulous!

Also, we have a feeling that you have a History test today. And you're trying to study now? On the bus? With the Brookfield boys climbing onto each other's shoulders to get to the emergency roof exit? And with Celia about to get on the bus at any moment? And you think that's going to make a difference!!!

That's really very amusing, Elizabeth. We like you for it.

You're perfect for our Society and we're very excited about having you join.

Yours sincerely,
The Manager
Society of People Who Are Definitely Going to Fail High School (And Most Probably Life as Well!)

A Letter To A Complete And Utter Stranger

Dear Complete and Utter Stranger,

The first thing that I have to say is that I hate porridge. I really hate it. And you know what? If you like porridge at all? I mean even the tiniest bit? I mean, say you were lost in the Himalayas, right, and you hadn't eaten anything except a Mars Bar for about seven years, right, and you're really cold and your fingers are all dropping off, right, and you look behind this rock, and there's this bowl of porridge?

Say you would even *think* about eating the porridge?

Well, JUST DON'T BOTHER WRITING TO ME, OK?

I don't want to hurt your feelings or anything, but I don't want to have anything to do with you.

I really hate porridge.

The second thing that I have to say is that *it's ok if you don't want to read this*. If you want to just tear it into tiny little pieces and throw it away? Or you want to tip sulphuric acid all over it, or whatever?

That's OK.

I'm only writing it because of Mr Botherit. He's our new English teacher and he seems really upset that the Art of Letter Writing is lost to the Internet generation, so he's going to rekindle the joy of the ENVELOPE. Next he's going to bring in a club and a sabre tooth tiger and rekindle the joy of the STONE AGE.

Anyway, but Mr Botherit also organized the letter exchange because he's upset that our school has nothing to do with your school. He said that if two schools are exactly three blocks away from each other

6

they should forge ties. I don't want to hurt your feelings or anything, but I think we've been OK so far without any tie forging. I think you've been OK without us too.

The good thing about this is that Mr Botherit doesn't seem to know that Mrs Cheerson, our old teacher? She gave us an essay to write over the holiday. It was on *To Kill a Mockingbird*, which I read and it was good, and I think it's stupid to spoil a good book by writing an essay on it. So I didn't do it.

Mr Botherit wrote these things on the board and he says we should put them in here. So I have to say them to you and I'm very sorry.

1. My Name: just look at the bottom of the letter, and it says it there.
2. My Interests: long-distance running, netball, making macrame plant holders (*not really*) (but really about the running and netball).
3. My Friends: my best friend is Celia Buckley. (But she's not at school today – she didn't get on the bus this morning. You might not think that's very important but that's because you don't know Celia Buckley.) My other best friend is my dog, Lochie.
4. My Holiday: I went skiing with my dad to Thredbo.

There are about twenty-five million other things on the list but this is boring and stupid. You don't care. You have probably put the sulphuric acid on this by now anyway and *all my words are being wasted.*

Yours sincerely,
Elizabeth Clarry

Dear Ms Clarry,

I know what you're planning to do right now. You're planning
to get the bus straight to Celia's place. Aren't you?

You're going to check that she's OK, right? And if she's had a
relapse of typhoid fever you're going to mop her brow and
bring her cans of Diet Coke, right? And if she's run away to
make a living playing her recorder on street corners then you're
going to buy her a tie-dyed rug to stand on, right?

The Manager
Best Friends Club

Dear Elizabeth,

I know just what you're going to do this afternoon. You're
going to do a 10k run, aren't you?

The Trail Run is just eight weeks away now. You want to
finish first, don't you? Or finish in the top ten? Or finish?

Don't you?

Yours ever,
The Society of High School Runners Who Aren't Very Good at
Long-Distance Running But Would Be if They Just Trained.

!!!! OVER HERE !!!! ELIZABETH !!! ON THE TABLE
HERE !!! A NOTE FOR YOU !!!

DEAR LIBBY,

THANK YOU FOR YOUR NOTE THIS MORNING. I
WOULD JUST LIKE TO SAY THAT IF YOUR LEGS GET

FROSTBITTEN AND PURPLE FROM NOT WEARING
STOCKINGS, AND YOUR FACE PEELS AWAY LEAVING
YOU WITH NOTHING BUT BRAINS AND BLOOD AND
EYEBALLS FROM NOT PUTTING ALOE ON IT, THEN
<u>DON'T COME CRYING TO ME</u>.

I HOPE YOUR FIRST DAY BACK AT SCHOOL WAS
GOOD.

I'M AT THE ALEXANDER TECHNIQUE CLASS
LEARNING HOW TO MAKE MY NECK STOP MAKING
THAT CRUNCHING SOUND WHEN I TURN AROUND.

IF YOU'RE BORED TONIGHT WHY DON'T YOU WRITE
DOWN EVERYTHING THAT COMES INTO YOUR MIND
WHEN YOU HEAR THE WORD TOOTHPASTE?

WITH LOTS OF LOVE FROM YOUR MUM

Dear Mum,

I'm going to bed now. I hope your neck has stopped
crunching.

My first day back was OK. But Celia wasn't there.

!!!

I went for a run over to her place and Mrs Buckley
says she climbed out of her bedroom window last night
and disappeared again. Mrs Buckley said she heard her
climbing out the window because she fell on top of
Benjamin's drum kit which he has in the garden so that
he can practise by moonlight. But Mrs Buckley just
pretended not to hear. She says we should all just
breathe in and out and stop stressing, and leave Celia
to figure out Celia's own thing.

Thank you for your exciting suggestion about how to
spend my night tonight.

9

Here is what comes into my mind when I hear the word TOOTHPASTE:

teeth.

Lots of love,
Elizabeth

A Letter From A Complete And Utter Stranger

Dear Elizabeth Clarry,

Actually I think porridge is cool. You probably just haven't had good porridge. It has to be steaming like a shower so it burns the tastebuds off of your tongue, and you have to tip a packet of brown sugar on top of it.

I wrote an essay on *To Kill A Mockingbird* last term. If you need it, I'll send it to you. I think the best way to forge ties between our schools is for us to **swap homework**. Have you ever done an assignment on the human immune system?

1. My Name: It's down the bottom. You can call me Chris if you want to but you can NEVER CALL ME TINA. If you do, I'll break your face.
2. My Interests: my butterfly collection (HA HA).
3. My Friends: My best friend is my cousin, Maddie. She lives in Double Bay and goes to Trinity Ladies College, so I've talked to people from *nice private schools* like yours before, so I'm used to you. A lot of people in my class aren't used to you so they were pissed off when Radison said we had to write letters, and some

10

wouldn't even take one of your letters out of the box. Tony Mason did take a letter but then he gave it straight back to Radison and said he could shove it up his arse. I don't know if he shoved it up his arse or not.

4. My Holiday: I stayed with my cousin Maddie in Double Bay and we watched videos and ate mango ripple ice cream. She has an ace stereo TV. You probably have one too, cos you're a nice private school girl.

5. My Boyfriend: You never said if you had a boyfriend or not. Do you? My boyfriend is called Derek. His main talent is whistling. He can whistle in perfect tune. His other main talent is his biceps. But he only flexes his muscles if he's completely hammered, like off his brain, cos he thinks he looks like a total nerd when he does.

Also, I've got two brothers and two sisters and they're all younger than me. So I'm the oldest.

What's the deal with 'long-distance running'? How long is a long distance anyway? And how come you like that?

Write back again cos I forgive you for being a nice private school girl.

Christina Kratovac

P.S. How come it's important that your friend Celia didn't get on the bus this morning? Is she like in a wheelchair or something?

A Letter To Someone Who Is Practically A Stranger

Dear Christina Kratovac,

I don't know what to do about the porridge.

Maybe we just shouldn't talk about it?

Thanks for writing back to me. I'm glad you got my letter and not that guy who told the teacher to shove it up his arse.

Long-distance running is like cross-country or marathon running, and long distances are different lengths – like the City to Surf is 14k, and a marathon is around 42.2k, and an ultra-marathon is to the North Pole and back. People always tell me I shouldn't run so far because I'm too young and my bones will fall to pieces. But I do it anyway – mainly because I love the bit when you finish and get to stop running. For example: the next race I'm going in is the Belongil Trail Run, which is 15k. Imagine stopping after 15k. It'll be fantastic.

A *VERY IMPORTANT THING* for you to know is that I'm NOT a nice private school girl. And I know I'm not, cause most of the other girls here *are* like that. They take clarinet lessons and go to pony club. And they do this thing whenever I'm talking to them where they blink their mascara'd lashes really quickly as if they need to take lots of little breaks from looking at me.

I'm writing this in Science and Mr Hoogenboom is going blah blah blah about the human skeleton. At the start of the lesson, before Mr Hoogenboom came in, this guy Martin Wilson turned around from the bench in front of mine and said, 'Elizabeth! You look *radiant*!'

So at first I think, 'Oh fantastic, Martin Wilson's got

a crush on me – now what?' (Martin Wilson's got orange hair which is crinkly like potato chips, and a chin like a cauliflower.)

But then David Corruthers looks around too and says, 'Man, is that *red* or what?'

So then I remember that my face is so red that my own dog doesn't recognize me any more. It's because I went skiing with my dad on the holidays and got sunburnt.

I can tell you right now that if I was a nice private school girl, I wouldn't've got a bright red face from going skiing. I'd've got a perfect golden tan like I'd dipped my head in a jar of honey.

Anyway, so Martin and David are staring at me like Mulder and Scully staring at the family of aliens they just discovered in the kitchen sink, when Mr Hoogenboom walks in.

And Martin calls out, 'Sir, look at Elizabeth's face! She's gonna get skin cancer, right? Maybe we should do a topic on *diseases* and use Elizabeth as our experiment?'

Mr Hoogenboom looks straight at my face. So does the entire class. Then everyone's calling out stuff like:

'How can you get sunburnt like that and still be *alive*?'

'Is she clinically dead, sir?'

Then Mr Hoogenboom clears his throat and Martin Wilson says, 'Do you have throat cancer, sir? Would you like to be one of the experiments too?'

The guys here are almost as bad as the girls, except stupider.

So anyway I really only have one friend here, that's Celia, and I promise you she is *most DEFINITELY not a nice private school girl*. She's kind of weird actually. She's always getting into trouble because she gets bored really really easily. So she always wants to try something new, like shaving her head or chopping down a tree or taking apart the kitchen so she can put it back together (she did that to my kitchen actually, and it took us six months to reconnect the dishwasher).

My mum says it's because Celia has an attention span the size of a sesame seed.

Celia's mum says it's because Celia's identity is unfurling itself slowly, like a tulip bud, and it's a breathtakingly beautiful thing to see.

Anyway, I'm kind of depressed today because Celia's run away again. She does that a lot but she usually at least calls me to say where she is. And she hasn't called yet. I'm scared that something bad will happen to her. My mum called Celia's mum and said, 'Why don't you tell the police?' but Celia's mum just said, 'Remember the tulip bud?' and told my mum to breathe in and out.

Sorry for making this letter so long. I hope you're not bored. I hope you write back. Tell me your brothers' and sisters' names if you want? I never met anyone with two brothers and two sisters.

From
Elizabeth

!! ELIZABETH !!

THERE IS PORRIDGE <u>ON THE STOVE FOR YOU.</u>

YOUR BLAZER IS IN A HEAP ON THE LIVING-ROOM FLOOR WHERE YOU LEFT IT LAST NIGHT.

I'LL TRY CALLING CELIA'S MUM AGAIN TODAY.

CALL ME AT WORK IF SHE SHOWS UP AT SCHOOL.

CAN YOU PEEL FOUR POTATOES WHEN YOU GET HOME FROM SCHOOL?

14

IF YOU ARE BORED WHILE PEELING THE POTATOES
YOU CAN SPEND THE TIME THINKING ABOUT THE
COLOUR <u>WHITE</u>. WHAT ARE SOME <u>REALLY WHITE</u>
<u>THINGS</u>?

SEE YOU TONIGHT,

MUM

P.S. YOUR FATHER CALLED YOU. (I THOUGHT YOU
SAID HE WAS FLYING BACK TO CANADA A WEEK
AGO? HE'S GOING TO TRY AND CALL AGAIN LATER
TONIGHT.)

Dear Mum,

Celia didn't show up at school. I don't know how come
Dad's still here.
    I'm taking Lochie for a run and I'll be back in an
hour for dinner.
    Here are the potatoes.
    I thought of something white: potatoes.

Love from Elizabeth

Dear Elizabeth,

A couple of weeks ago, Celia phoned in the middle of the night
to suggest you meet in the park for a midnight feast. A week
ago, Celia talked you into skipping Science, to go and tour a
chocolate factory instead. And a few days ago, Celia got you to

15

help her plant an avocado tree in her backyard, as the first step in creating her own, personal ecosystem.

Just a few seconds ago, what did you do? You peeled some potatoes.

Gee, Elizabeth, things are really looking up for you now that your best friend's not around, aren't they?

Yours,
Best Friends Club

A Letter From A Stranger

Dear Elizabeth,

I CAN'T BELIEVE YOU HAVE A TEACHER CALLED MR HOOGENBOOM.

Were you for real about that or were you just taking the piss?

If we had a teacher here with a name like Mr Hoogenboom, he'd be dead by now. Seriously, people here wouldn't let him live.

I'm sorry I called you a nice private school girl. I believe you now that you're not one of them. You don't really sound like one of them. How come you're at that school then?

But you did go skiing in the holidays, which sounds kind of private school. I'm sorry your face went red. You should've used sunscreen or it's true about the skin cancer. I'm very sorry but it's true. You'll get it. My Uncle Rosco had skin cancer on the end of his nose. It cost him five thousand dollars to have it surgically removed. (My dad said he'd have done it with his

16

power saw for a case of beer, which Uncle Rosco didn't think was very funny.) Auntie Belinda's always getting moles cut off her arms too. Actually, I don't really think that's cos of skin cancer, I think it's because she wants arms without moles.

Those guys in your science class sound like walruses. I think you should punch Martin Wilson right in his cauliflower chin.

That must be really hard for you having your best friend run away all the time. You must be worried a lot. Plus you must miss her. I hope she's called you by now, or come back.

It's funny that your friend runs away, and you go running like a billion kilometres just for fun. It makes you both a bit weird. I think you should listen to people who tell you not to run long distances, and not just because your bones will fall to pieces. Because you're out of your mind. 15ks? You're insane.

Anyway, I'm sorry to make jokes about your friend running away. That's a serious thing.

Actually, Celia sounds a bit like my cousin Maddie. Maddie's always getting into trouble and running away too, but it's not cos she's bored. It's always cos of *love.*

Maddie's always falling in love with a different guy. Except the different guys are always the same. I mean, they're always kind of wild. She really goes for the wild type. And they always get her into trouble, like going to the casino all night, or they get her to run away to Surfers' with them. Then her dad says she can't see them any more and she gets into even more trouble climbing out of their top floor apartment window and trying to slide down the drainpipe.

If you really want to know about my brothers and sisters I'll tell you. Do you really? OK, I'm going to tell you right now, and if you only asked to be polite or something, you should skip the next bit. OK?

Well, first there's my brother, Nick. He's twelve, eats nothing except raw spaghetti, and hasn't said a word for the last two years. Well, he has said about five words but only when I got hold of his neck and squeezed it till his face went purple. Then he spoke until I let go. But only in swear words. He used to be kind of like a friend of mine – well, he used to be my slave, anyway, because he worshipped me when he was small.

Then there's Renee. She's eight and she's an angel. She's smart too – last year my grandmother had a heart attack right in front of Renee's eyes, when they were alone in the house, and Renee called emergency services and got an ambulance and SAVED GRAND-MA'S LIFE. Cool, huh? For a seven year old. She also remembered to switch off the stove where Grandma was boiling rhubarb so it wouldn't all boil away into mulch.

Then there's Robbo, who's five, and he's the devil.

Last there's the baby, Lauren, and she just turned one. She can run but she can't walk, because if she slows down to a walk she loses her balance and tips over sideways. She can also talk but only in a completely unknown language.

My mum had two miscarriages between Robbo and Lauren too, so I guess there'd be seven of us, and this letter would go on for ever.

My dad came over here from Slovenia when he was about sixteen, and he met my mum picking grapes up at Mudgee. Mum's family's Italian.

Sorry, I accidentally started telling you my whole family history. Anyway, I can hear Derek coming (he's whistling Pearl Jam's *Alive* and it sounds *exactly like the original*; you have to admit that it's a real talent and I don't see why they don't let him in the school band) so I'm gonna tell Radison that I've got a headache and get out of here.

See ya.
Don't forget to write back.
Christina

Dear Ms Clarry,

I see you have a pimple just beneath your nose today.

That's a good start and we'd like to compliment you on that. Teenagers are supposed to have pimples.

BUT YOU KNOW WHAT?

That's the MOST DISGUSTING ZIT WE HAVE EVER SEEN.

And you know what else? *Real* teenagers cleanse their faces every day to avoid that kind of thing.

Get into the fridge, and put your head in a paper bag.

All the best,
The Association of Teenagers

!!! ELIZABETH !!!

I'M NOT COMING HOME TILL LATE TONIGHT. GET YOURSELF A BARBECUED CHICKEN AT THE FISH AND CHIP SHOP AND DO SOME FROZEN VEGETABLES.

(ON THE WAY TO GETTING THE CHICKEN YOU COULD TAKE LOCHIE TO THE VET FOR HIS INJECTION. THAT COULD BE FUN. YOU NEVER KNOW WHO YOU MIGHT MEET IN A VET'S WAITING ROOM.)

YOUR DAD CALLED ME AT WORK YESTERDAY LOOKING FOR YOU. I TOLD HIM YOU HADN'T FINISHED HIGH SCHOOL YET SO WHAT WOULD YOU BE DOING IN AN ADVERTISING AGENCY?

HE SAYS YOU HAVEN'T PHONED HIM BACK. CAN YOU CALL HIM AT HIS SYDNEY NUMBER BECAUSE I DON'T WANT HIM CALLING ME ANY MORE.

HAVE A NICE DAY.

LOVE FROM YOUR MUM

P.S. HAVE YOU HEARD FROM CELIA YET?

Mum,

There's leftover chicken if you want it.

I called Dad and he wants to take me to dinner on the weekend.

I called Celia's mum and she told me to take it easy and breathe more. But she seemed a bit surprised that I hadn't heard from Celia myself yet.

See ya,
Elizabeth

Dear Elizabeth,

Very well, Celia has been gone, without a word, for a week.

But you know perfectly well that in Celia-time a week is no more than a microsecond.

In Celia-time, your watch will say 'tick', you'll take a spaceship to the moon, rappel down a crater, have a party with the locals, and when you get back to Earth, your watch will say, for the second time: tick.

Remember when Celia's mother arrived at school on a Wednesday afternoon to take Celia on a spontaneous camping trip? She returned on a Thursday, one month later (they got lost in a wood), and she couldn't BELIEVE that the sandwich in her locker was growing toadstools. ('But I just put that in there yesterday!')

In Celia's mind, in Celia-time, a week is a microblip. A week is a tiny squidge of time, the size of a toothpaste cap.

There is nothing in the world to make you worry.

Yours faithfully,
The Director
Take a Deep Breath and Calm Down Society

Dear Elizabeth,

A lot can happen in a microblip, and especially a Celia-week microblip. Celia can crash her spaceship, break her ribs on the bottom of the crater, and get ptomaine poisoning from the alien's hors d'oeuvres . . .

Anything can happen with Celia around.

And if anything can happen when Celia is around, anything can happen when she's not.

21

She could never come back.

If we were you, Elizabeth, we'd be very worried.

Yours

Best Friends Club

P.S. Another thing: in Celia-time, a week might be a microblip. But how long is a school week in YOUR boring time, your get-out-of-bed and go-to-school, make excuses for not doing homework, take the bus home and not do homework, take Lochie for a run and go to bed, and then, oh hey, it's another day, hooray, let's get-out-of-bed and go-to-school time? How long is a week in your time, Elizabeth? A year?

Letter To A Stranger

Dear Christina,

Thanks for your letter, I really liked it, and I'm really glad you told me about your family. It wasn't boring at all, it was cool. I haven't got any brothers or sisters (except for a stepbrother who I've never met) and I'd LOVE to have one, so if you have any to spare send one to me in your next letter. The baby sounds cute, for example. And that smart one, Renee, she sounds useful to have around in case of emergencies.

I'm writing this in Maths because I don't believe in coordinate geometry. I don't think it's healthy really.

For one thing, it's bad for my brain. I know it's bad for my brain because it gives me a headache. I have a headache right now, and there's no reason for me to have a headache. I haven't been bashing my head

22

against a brick wall or anything, for instance. Also, I don't know why I have to find out the midpoint between two dots on a piece of paper. Excuse me, but who needs to know? And if they do need to know why can't they do it themselves? Or just look it up in the back of the book? THE ANSWERS ARE THERE.

For another thing, everyone in this entire room's sick; they're all coughing and sneezing and making disgusting snorting, snotty noises, and the guy who sits next to me just coughed and I saw a little splat of gooey green stuff land on my Maths book. I don't know if anything as disgusting as that has ever happened to you.

So I'm not going to do Maths. Anyway, I'm depressed. Sorry if I always sound depressed. It's for these reasons:

1. Celia still hasn't called me. I'm scared. I don't know where she is. It's been over a week now. And nobody seems to think there's anything to worry about except me.
2. Disgusting, gooey green stuff just landed on my Maths book right in front of my eyes.
3. I have a sore throat.
4. I didn't train this morning and I want to train six days a week because the Trail Run's coming up soon and I really want to do well in it. Plus if I don't run for a few days I start to feel crazy and depressed.
5. I phoned my dad this morning – he's still in Sydney. He was supposed to go back to Canada ages ago. (He lives in Canada with his second wife and her son – he left my mum and ran off with this woman when I was a baby.) He wants to take me out to dinner on the weekend,

because he has *something exciting to tell me.* I suppose that's not a reason to be depressed, because maybe the exciting thing'll be good. Like maybe he finally wants to take me to Canada with him. (I've never been there and I've never even met the second wife or her son, can you believe that? I mean I'm his only daughter, aren't I?)

But I hate going out to dinner with my dad. I can never think of anything to say. And you can see him sitting there trying to figure out really *teenage* stuff to talk about. And we always go somewhere posh and he gets me a glass of wine, even though I hate wine, and then we have conversations where he goes something like, 'Elizabeth? How about the nose on this shiraz, hmm?' and I think he's talking about the waiter or something, so I look around for the one with the big nose, and he goes, 'I mean the wine, darling' and then I feel stupid.

Then he goes, 'Have a sniff of it, what does it smell like to you, sweetheart?'

And I go, 'Um. Wine.'

And he goes, 'Mmm. Yes, but what else? Come on!'

'Um. Red wine.'

'Nothing else? You can't smell a fruit in there? Come on now, what kind of a fruit is there?'

'Apples?'

'Apples? Really? Interesting. I don't get that myself. You don't, by any chance, get strawberries, do you?'

'Um.'

'Raspberries?'

'I guess.' (Even though it smells exactly like red wine.)

'Blackberries?'

'Maybe.' (Even though it still smells exactly like red wine.)

'Nutmeg?'

'Mmm.' (What's nutmeg smell like anyhow?)

'That's it! That's a girl! It's delirious, isn't it? It's like summer pudding and Christmas cake all mixed up into one glorious flavour celebration, isn't it? Isn't it?!'

Then he's really pleased with himself because he thinks he's taking care of my *cultural education*.

And then he always asks how my mum's doing and as soon as I start to answer he looks around the room for a waiter and asks for another bottle of wine or a whiskey on the rocks or something.

Anyway, so that's what it's like going to dinner with my dad.

I hope you're having a good day and eating something else besides porridge for breakfast, because I think it's probably bad for your brain, and I'm sorry about that, I know you like it, but that's it.

From,
Elizabeth

!! ELIZABETH !!

LIBBY, I HOPE YOU FEEL BETTER THIS MORNING. I MADE EXTRA PORRIDGE FOR YOU, AND A NICE HOT LEMON DRINK WHICH WILL BE GOOD FOR YOUR THROAT. WHILE YOU'RE DRINKING IT YOU COULD THINK ABOUT HOW YOU WOULD FEEL IF YOU WERE AT A HOLIDAY RESORT WHICH IS ENTIRELY UNDERWATER

SO EVERYONE HAS TO WEAR OXYGEN TANKS AND
WATERPROOF MASCARA. HAVE A GOOD DAY GETTING
AN EDUCATION!

LOVE FROM YOUR MUM

Dear Mum,

I'm not going to school today. I'm going back to bed. I
will die very soon.

Thinking about underwater holiday resorts makes
my head feel worse, so I don't want to do it, thank you
all the same.

Elizabeth

DEAR LIBBY,

I HOPE YOUR COLD FEELS BETTER. I'M IN THE LIVING-
ROOM AND I DIDN'T WANT TO WAKE YOU SO I'M
PUTTING THIS NOTE UNDER YOUR DOOR. DO YOU
WANT SOME DINNER?

LOVE, MUM

Dear Mum,

It's not a cold, it's PNEUMONIA. I'm writing this at
2.30 a.m. and I'm going to put it on your door because
it might be the last time you'll ever hear from me. Both

26

nostrils are stuffed and my throat's about to disappear completely, and when that happens I don't really see how breathing will be possible. So I guess I'll be dead when I see you next.

So, BYE MUM.
Love from Elizabeth

NOTE FOR ELIZABETH !!! FOR WHEN SHE WAKES UP !!!! LOOK HERE ON TOP OF YOUR CLOCK RADIO, LIBBY!!!

I HOPE YOU FEEL BETTER TODAY. PLEASE RING ME AT WORK IF YOU ARE DEAD.
TAKE VITAMIN C'S (IN THE BOTTLE NEXT TO THE TISSUES JUST OVER THERE).
PUT VICKS VAPOUR RUB ON YOUR CHEST (ON THE FLOOR NEXT TO YOUR BED).

LOVE FROM YOUR MUM

P.S. I'M SORRY I THOUGHT IT WAS JUST A COLD WHEN IT'S PNEUMONIA.

P.P.S. ONE THING YOU MIGHT DO TODAY IS THINK ABOUT CREATIVE WAYS TO DESCRIBE YOUR SYMPTOMS. E.G. IF YOU HAVE A HEADACHE, DOES IT FEEL LIKE DRUMS BEATING AGAINST YOUR FOREHEAD? IF YOU HAVE A SORE THROAT, DOES IT FEEL LIKE ANTS CRAWLING AROUND YOUR THROAT? BUT ONLY DO THIS IF YOU'RE FEELING UP TO IT OF COURSE.

Dear Ms Clarry,

Here's your perfect opportunity to climb into the fridge. Lying around under your Little Mermaid duvet all day must surely highlight how HOPELESS you are!

May we remind you that the only time you ever throw up is when you have the flu? Never from getting smashed off your brain. Ever been DRUNK, Elizabeth? Oh no, that's right! The only time you drink is when your FATHER gives you a glass of wine! That's so impressive!

You haven't even SEEN marijuana, let alone experimented with the hard drugs that you're SUPPOSED to be using.

What are you waiting for? You know you're a waste of space.

Yours sincerely,
The Association of Teenagers

Dear Ms Clarry,

Another thing. Most teenagers are supposed to have heaps of friends to do all the drinking and drug-taking and vandalizing with. And to go to parties with, and movies, and dance parties.

Apparently, you only have ONE friend and she's disappeared off the face of the Earth!

You really ARE a waste of space!

The Association of Teenagers

Dear Elizabeth,

But if your one friend were here she could be mopping your brow and squeezing you fresh orange juice. You wouldn't have to drag yourself out of bed to fetch aspirin from the kitchen, and you wouldn't have to watch *The Bold and the Beautiful* to stop yourself dying of boredom.

Remember that time when you were nine years old and had a fever? And Celia decided to cure your fever by getting you to climb out the bedroom window, dressing you up in a scarf and coat, and making you run laps around the local football field? (She'd heard you have to sweat out a fever.)

It turned out the fever was the beginning of measles, and running around a field in a coat was not the cure after all.

But the surprise was how much you loved running around the field, even with a fever – and you haven't stopped running since.

Sincerely,
Memory Trigger Society

Elizabeth,

Of course, right now the only thing that's running is your nose.

Cold Hard Truth Association

Dear Elizabeth,

Your dad sounds *exactly* like my Uncle Rosco. That's my cousin Maddie's father. Is your mum like my Auntie

Belinda? She's always getting bits zapped off, like moles off her arm, and eyebrows off her face, and cellulite off her thighs. She's got black painted-on eyebrows, which look like she used a black crayon and pressed really hard. And her nails are so long that they practically drag along the carpet behind her. And she's always carrying the cat around, which is a big fat lazy fluffy pile of shit, and then going, 'Oh LORD, CAT HAIRS, on my CASHMERE!'

Which you'd think she'd've worked out already and would just stop carrying the cat around.

I agree totally about coordinate geometry, and basically everything else in Maths altogether. I think you should just copy the answers straight out from the back of the book and then spend your Maths lessons writing to me. OK?

I'm very sorry about the green goobey landing on your Maths book. Nothing as disgusting as that has ever happened to me.

I talked to Maddie on the phone last night and she's kind of depressed cos Uncle Rosco and Auntie Belinda are going away for the weekend and leaving her alone and she hasn't got a boyfriend at the moment so it's wasted. And I can't go over there cos I've gotta help at my mum's shop this weekend (she's a florist). This is the longest Maddie's been without a boyfriend (six weeks) since Year 7, which at least keeps her out of trouble but gets kind of boring hearing her going on about it. And I'm not allowed to talk about Derek cos it just makes her more depressed and she says it's insensitive.

Has your friend Celia turned up yet? Has she called you yet? Is your throat better? It's bad that you were depressed. I'm going to tape an M&M down the bottom of this letter to try and cheer you up. I hope it works.

Gotta go cos I'm actually supposed to be doing a History exam right now.

How was the dinner with your dad? I thought of what you should do if he pulls that shit on you with the wine again. Tell him it smells exactly like cow manure and take a swig straight from the bottle.

Love,
Christina

M&M—

Dear Elizabeth,

Did you get my letter? I wrote it a week ago but it might've got lost. I hope I didn't offend you in my last letter. Do you hate M&Ms or something? Maybe you have that porridge thing about them too?

It's been an OK week, but Maddie's still depressed, which is getting kind of boring. Not that I mean I think you're boring when you're depressed. I think you've got a reason to be, I mean with your best friend vanished and everything. But Maddie's not exactly a nun. She's had 326 boyfriends since she was eleven.

You still haven't told me if you've got a boyfriend or not. Have you? And if you haven't now, who was your last boyfriend?

Write back SOON cos I'm worried that you're mad at me.

Love,
Christina

Dear Ms Clarry,

Excuse me, but what's going on here?

Maybe we weren't clear enough about our problems with you.

You've had plenty of time to climb into the refrigerator and YOU'RE STILL NOT THERE. You're out there in the world!

You're sitting on bus seats and walking around shopping centres and EVERYBODY CAN SEE YOU!

You're writing letters to that Christina person PRETENDING THAT YOU'RE A REAL TEENAGER. She'll work it out soon, Elizabeth. She's not stupid.

You leave us with no other choice, Ms Clarry. We are going to have to cut to the chase.

Ms Clarry, you have never had a boyfriend.

Now, perhaps you will understand. Now, perhaps you will think of other respectable teenagers, and what you are doing to the teenage image, and you will hop right into the lettuce cooler and stay there.

Yours sincerely,
The Association of Teenagers

!!! ELIZABETH !!! OVER HERE!! ON THE FRIDGE!!

KEEP <u>VERY</u> WARM AT SCHOOL TODAY. I DON'T THINK YOU WERE DRESSED WARMLY ENOUGH YESTERDAY. WEAR A <u>SWEATER AND LONG UNDERWEAR</u> UNDER YOUR UNIFORM. ALSO, GRANDMA'S OLD PURPLE SHAWL IS ON THE COUCH. TAKE IT AND PUT IT OVER YOUR LEGS.

THERE IS A SACK OF ORANGES IN THE FRIDGE.
TAKE THEM ALL TO SCHOOL WITH YOU AND EAT THEM.

LOVE,
YOUR
MUM

Dear Mum,

I won't be able to move my arms if I wear a sweater and
long underwear under my uniform. Grandma's purple
shawl has pine needles all over it from when we used it
as a picnic blanket last summer. I'll take one orange.
Thanks.

Celia's mum called after you'd gone, while I was in
the shower. I called her back. She wanted to know if I'd
heard from Celia yet. When I said no she breathed a lot
for a while, in and out.

See you later,
Elizabeth

Dear Elizabeth,

We hear you've misplaced your best friend.

Just out of interest, you might want to locate her pretty soon
if you want to retain your membership in this club.

In this club, you see, what we do is, we hang out with our
best friends.

You remember? You and Celia used to be very good at that
when you were small. That time, for example, when Celia
decided you should live in her tree house?

Your mother had come by to pick you up after a Sunday at Celia's and you both came running to ask if you could move into the tree house, please.

Your mother came into the kitchen and laughed and said, 'Maybe one day.'

And Celia's mother, from the frying pan, said, 'Well, why not today?'

'Well, I don't really think—'

'Well, I don't see why not—'

'Perhaps when they're a bit older—'

Both of their voices were getting sterner; Celia's mother was burning the onions in the frying pan and your mother was waving her hands surreptitiously at the smoke.

'Oh, come on, they could take sleeping bags, it will be sweet—'

'It's a school night and it's the middle of winter, for heaven's sake!'

'But that's what children do! They move into tree houses! It's an exquisite idea!'

Celia and you were on the floor, trying not to giggle, and playing with her little brother's toy cars (the kind that you pull back along the linoleum to build up speed and then let go). Celia's mother was wrenching open the jammed kitchen window to let the smoke out of the room. Your mother was coughing dramatically, and jumping when the toy cars hit her ankles.

'What kind of a tree house is this anyway? Who built the tree house?'

'Celia did!'

'Celia is seven years old!'

Celia's mum was now climbing onto the counter to get more leverage at the window and your mother was climbing onto the kitchen table to avoid the speeding cars.

'Celia is a very advanced child.'

'What's it made out of, this advanced child's tree house?'

'Oh, wood, I suppose.'

'Oh, wood, you suppose?'

'I'm sure it is perfectly sound.'

'You're sure! Have you SEEN this house? Do you know what tree this house is in?'

That was when they both turned on Celia and demanded, 'What TREE is this house in?'

And Celia explained: 'I haven't built it yet.'

Then you both decided to go and ride your bikes and left them standing there – your mother on the kitchen table, Celia's mother on the kitchen counter – their mouths wide open in shock.

Remember hanging out with your best friend? Do you remember how to do that?

The Manager
Best Friends Club

Dear Christina,

I'm really sorry about not writing back for so long. I wasn't offended at all by your letter, and I love M&Ms. I loved the M&M you sent me so much that I kept it and now it's glued to an ice lolly and standing on my dressing table.

I've been away from school 'cause I had a really bad flu. I was throwing up and feverish and everything. And my body was aching like I'd spent a week doing sit-ups. I only got your two letters yesterday.

I don't think my mother is very much like your Auntie Belinda. I don't think she's had any bits zapped off her, and her eyebrows don't look like crayon. But she writes with purple and green pens, and she waves her hands around when she's thinking, so she's always got purple and green scribbles on her face. She hasn't got long nails that drag along the floor behind her either. She keeps her nails really short because she's frightened of scratching her eyes out when she's putting in her contact lenses.

And she doesn't carry a cat around, because we haven't got a cat. We've got a dog. But he's a hyperactive collie and my mother's a small woman.

Actually, I think maybe my dad should have married someone like your Auntie Belinda instead of my mum. I don't really know why they got together in the first place. Dad took me to dinner last night (I had to cancel last weekend's dinner because of my flu), so I found out what the exciting news is. This is what happened . . .

Well, first of all I was still getting over my flu so I had a kind of hazy feeling. Like I was walking around inside a big bubble.

My mum said I had to wear three T-shirts and a jumper and a scarf. So we're at this slick restaurant in Double Bay where all the women are basically dressed in their silk underwear, and I'm sitting there like the Abominable Snowman.

And Dad's all excited and mysterious, going: 'Bet you can't wait to hear my news, huh?'

So I'm being polite and saying, 'No, Dad, I really can't wait.'

And he's doing his wine thing, you know: 'Have a try of this, Liz, it's a really elegant little number, what do you think of the nose, hmm?'

So I try your advice. I say, 'It smells like cow manure.'

And you know what happens? He gets wild with happiness, and practically shouts, 'You're RIGHT!' And then he's doing this little dance in his seat, going: 'Cow manure! Of course! That delicious *farmyard* quality, hmm? The whole stables and horses and old leather thing, hmm? That wonderful boiled cabbage and compost heap flavour, hmm?'

And then he calls out for ANOTHER BOTTLE, so we can share THAT ONE TOO, and he fills my glass to the brim and says, 'Drink up!'

And he's sitting there with this huge stupid grin on his face like we've had some kind of magical father–daughter breakthrough.

And I'm sitting there thinking he wants me to *drink* cow shit, boiled cabbage and compost heap?

It made me feel quite sick actually, so I couldn't do your next bit of advice and take a swig from the bottle.

But then he tells me the news.

It's this. He is going to live in Sydney for the next year.

If you're thinking 'big deal' you're exactly right.

Big deal.

He works for this airline and he usually comes back from Canada for a few weeks every year. But this time he's going to be stationed here for a year.

So what?

And he's not even bringing his family over, which might have made it interesting. Do you realize I have a stepmother and a stepbrother who I've never met? But they're going to stay in Canada for a year without him, which seems like a long time don't you reckon?

And my mum's going to be *really* happy when she hears about this.

Anyway, I should go, I wrote too much again, sorry.

Celia's still not back, thanks for asking. I can't really concentrate on anything, because I'm worrying about her all the time.

I hope your cousin Maddie has a new boyfriend by now. I hope you don't have the flu that everyone in the world has.

Write soon.

Love,
Elizabeth

ELIZABETH !!!

I'M AT THE COUNCIL MEETING BECAUSE I WANT TO PROTEST AGAINST THEIR NEW BY-LAW. DO YOU REALIZE THEY HAVE PROHIBITED ROLLERBLADING IN THE SHOPPING CENTRE? WHAT IF I WANTED TO ROLLERBLADE TO THE SUPERMARKET? IT'S DISGRACEFUL.

CELIA'S MUM CALLED ME AT WORK TODAY. SHE SAID SHE WANTED TO KNOW WHERE I DID MY YOGA. I TOLD HER I HAVEN'T DONE YOGA FOR SEVEN YEARS. I'M A BIT WORRIED ABOUT HER.

SEE YOU LATER,

MUM

Mum,

I hope the council meeting went well. Do you actually know what rollerblading is?

The principal called me into his office to see him today, asking if I know where Celia is. He said that he has called her mother but has 'not been entirely satisfied with the response'. I told him he should breathe in and out more, and he looked absolutely terrified.

I just called Celia's mum myself and she said everyone's taking this way too seriously and she was only interested in yoga because of a slight twinge in her left knee.

There's leftover frozen pizza if you're still hungry. I'm going to bed now.

See you tomorrow.

Elizabeth

ELIZABETH !!!

THERE ARE SIX MILLION WHITE SOCKS IN THE LAUNDRY BASKET IF YOU NEED THEM.

HAVE A NICE DAY.

I'M GOING TO TRY AND TALK CELIA'S MUM INTO CALLING THE POLICE TODAY.

YOUR MUM

Letter From A Total Stranger

Dear Elizabeth,

I am not Christina. I'm Derek, her boyfriend. She says you know all about me and she says you know about my whistling talent. If you know any agents who are interested in whistling, give us a call.

She asked me to write to you and say that she's got the flu but she hasn't forgotten you and she'll write soon.

Also she asked me to ask if your friend Celia showed up or not. Has she?

Plus she asked me to send you an M&M but I haven't got any. Sorry. So I'm sending you this blade of grass instead.

BLADE OF GRASS —

Yours faithfully,
Derek Carmichael

Mum,

I just ran around to Celia's. Her mum is acting very strange, but she still says she won't call the police. She is spending most of her time banging on Ben's drums in the garden. She says it's releasing the energy that is causing the twinge in her knee.

I'm worried about Celia.

Elizabeth

ELIZABETH,

I AM THINKING ABOUT CALLING THE POLICE MYSELF.
  EITHER THAT OR FAMILY SERVICES. WHAT'S WRONG
WITH THAT WOMAN?

                                        LOVE,
                                     YOUR MUM

P.S. YOUR FATHER PHONED ME AT WORK YESTERDAY
AND SAID HE'S STAYING IN SYDNEY FOR THE NEXT
YEAR. YOU NEVER TOLD ME THAT.

Dear Christina,

I know you won't get this right away, if you're not back
at school, but maybe Derek will see it and take it to you?
I'm really sorry you have the flu. I hope I didn't give it
to you through my letter-writing somehow.

I know we haven't even met each other but I kind of
miss you. I don't know what to do. I feel like I'm the
only one who cares about Celia, but I don't know what
I should do about it. Where is she? What if she's sick or
lost or dead or something? What if somebody's taken
her?

I really don't know what I'd do without her. I don't
feel like doing anything right now.

I'm sorry to go on like this. I don't know who elsc to
talk to.

Hope you feel better.

                                        Love,
                                     Elizabeth

41

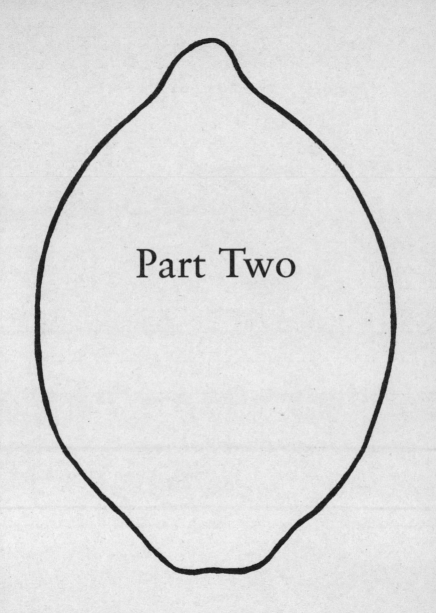

Part Two

'Byron Bay at dusk – a tropical dream!' Photograph by Daniel L. Lewisham. Postcard produced by Geelong Graphics.

Lizzy!!!!!

Hi! Wish you were here! I've joined a circus !!!!!!!!!!!!!!!! I'm just sewing up the holes in the tent at the moment, but they say they'll teach mc how to be an acrobat soon. You have to come and see the show some time!!!!!!!!
 Miss ya heaps.

Love,
Celia

P.S. If you see my mother, can you tell her where I am?

Mum,

LOOK AT THE POSTCARD ON THE FRIDGE DOOR UNDERNEATH THE PIG MAGNET.
 She's joined the circus.
 I phoned Celia's mum as soon as I got it.
 She said: 'Well, of course! The *circus*! What were we thinking?'

45

Like Celia had been down at the corner store the whole time and no one had thought of looking there.

I'm taking Lochie to the park for a run.

See ya

Love,
Elizabeth

ELIZABETH !!!

<u>OF COURSE</u>, THE CIRCUS!

I GUESS IT JUST SLIPPED OUR MINDS. CRAZY, HUH?

I'M GLAD CELIA'S OK, LIZ. BUT RUNNING AWAY TO JOIN THE CIRCUS? DOES SHE THINK SHE'S IN AN ENID BLYTON BOOK?

MAYBE I SHOULD PHONE FAMILY SERVICES ANYWAY.

YOUR DAD PHONED ME <u>AGAIN</u>. HE SAYS HE'S GOT A PLACE IN DOUBLE BAY FOR THE NEXT YEAR, BUT HE'S NOT BRINGING VERONICA OR HER SON. WHY ISN'T HE BRINGING THEM?

DOESN'T VERONICA WORK FOR THE SAME AIRLINE?

ANYWAY, CONGRATULATIONS ON FINDING YOUR FRIEND.

LOTS OF LOVE,
YOUR MUM

Dear Christina,

Guess what? I got a postcard from Celia. She's ALIVE.

Sorry. I hope you're alive too. Thank you very very

much for getting Derek to write to me. That was such a nice thing to do, especially when you were sick. I hope you're better now, I mean I hope you haven't dropped dead from the flu. It was the worst flu that I ever had. I hope it wasn't the worst flu you ever had.

I don't mean that I hope you're always getting really bad flus, I just mean I hope you didn't get it so bad.

Can you tell Derek thanks too? And I'm sending a twig for him from our apple tree. I took about three hours to choose the best one so I hope he appreciates it. And I'm sending a Smartie plus an M&M for you. You have to get someone to blindfold you and then you have to taste them and choose which one is best. Tell me which one you choose in your next letter. Then I'll tell you if you gave the correct answer.

Anyway, I got the postcard from Celia and I just burst into tears as soon as I saw it. I thought I was going to go crazy. It's been like Celia was just dead in an alley somewhere and no one gave a flying banana, except you. Sorry about saying 'flying banana' just then. It was an accident. My mother says it, and it's a really stupid thing to say.

Except for the 'flying' part of it. There's nothing wrong with that. FLYING. It's a really nice word. I always wanted to be able to fly. I know everyone wants that, but I think I wanted it *especially*. I mean, like, more than other people. (My mum says she wants to win the lottery more than most other people too, so she's shocked whenever it doesn't happen, even when she hasn't bought a lottery ticket.)

I don't mean flying aeroplanes or helicopters or kites

or whatever. I mean actually flying, you know just taking a step up into the sky.

Did you ever read this book about Ah-Mee and Tubby the Elephant? They make paper lanterns together. Then one day, Tubby the Elephant decides he wants to make a birthday present for Ah-Mee. So he gets a HUGE pile of paper, and an ENORMOUS pot of glue. And some kind of sticks, I guess. I don't remember. Anyway, he builds the sticks into a frame, then he covers it with paper, and he glues it all up. And he has to get some GINORMOUS pile of wax I guess, however you make candles, you know? And he builds an enormous, beautiful candle. Then he puts it inside the giant paper lantern.

Then Ah-Mee turns up and Tubby says, 'Happy Birthday!' and lights the candle. But it's such a big lantern that it starts to float upwards, so Tubby holds onto it, and so does Ah-Mee and *they go flying into the sky*. Then they just fly around for a while. It's cool.

Ever since I read that book I've wanted a giant paper lantern for my birthday.

Christina, I just want you to know that it's my birthday on March the 17th, which is St Patrick's day, so it's easy to remember. Just watch out for people wearing green. It's ages away so there's plenty of time for you to start collecting paper and candle wax if for any reason you wanted to collect paper and candle wax.

I keep forgetting what I was talking about.

Oh yeah, Celia.

The postcard was from Byron Bay and YOU'RE NOT GOING TO BELIEVE WHERE SHE'S BEEN ALL THIS TIME.

You want to try and guess? I'll give you some space to try and guess.

You can write your guesses down in that space if you want.

Maybe I should wait till the next letter and then tell you? Maybe I could make it like some TV series and show scenes from next week's letter?

No. That's stupid. I hate those shows.

I'll just tell you where she's been.

SHE JOINED THE CIRCUS.

Maybe I should give you some space to get over that information.

I hope you're over it now.

She said that they've got her sewing up the holes in the tents at the moment, but they're gonna teach her how to be an acrobat soon. I can't believe that while I'm doing English essays, she's sewing up holes in a circus tent.

Actually, I really can't believe it. She failed sewing classes last year because she couldn't even sew a button onto a piece of black cloth.

(I couldn't do it either but I wrote a letter saying I didn't believe that girls should have to do any sewing at all in their whole life, considering the history of discrimination against women.) (I tried doing the same thing in English the other day – our new teacher found out that we were supposed to write an essay on *To Kill a Mockingbird*. He said he didn't see the connection between the history of discrimination against women and writing an essay on *To Kill a Mockingbird*.)

So anyway, I hope it's not very important if the holes in the circus tent don't get sewn up properly. I mean, I hope it doesn't mean the lions will escape or anything.

I *can* believe that Celia's going to learn to be an acrobat. When we were little one of her favourite games was climbing up the mulberry tree in our backyard, then running as fast as she could along the fence, jumping onto the next-door neighbour's shed and sliding halfway across the roof. I did it in bare feet one summer day and got my feet full of splinters from the wooden fence, and huge burn blisters from the tin roof. Celia got so good at it that one time she slid right across the roof and fell off the other edge. She got a broken arm from that.

Another thing she liked to do was to stand up on the swings in her backyard, and get me to stand up on the same swing, but opposite her, so we were facing each other with our feet in a row. Then we had to swing as hard as we could, to try and get it to swing right over the top and around. Luckily, we never made it. We were trying to do that one time while Celia's arm was still broken from falling off the tin roof. So she couldn't really hold on properly, so she fell off and broke her other arm.

Well, I guess I should go. My dad's living in Sydney now, he's got a place in Double Bay so he'll probably call soon and want to do fun father/daughter things with me. *Fabulous.*

Love,
Elizabeth

Memo From the Desk of Albert Clarry

Hey there Elizabeth!

Imagine my being able to send memos to you from my office right here in Sydney!

This is my first day and it's exciting to be living in my home town, if only for a short time. To celebrate, perhaps I could take you to dinner this Thursday? Is a school night OK with you again? What about somewhere *really* snazzy? Would that be cool for you?

I'll phone as it gets closer.

Take care,
Dad

ELIZABETH !!!

I AM TAKING CELIA'S MOTHER TO MY AROMATHERAPY MAN TONIGHT.

I SPOKE TO HER ON THE PHONE TODAY AND I THINK SHE IS SUFFERING FROM POST-TRAUMATIC STRESS SYNDROME. SHE SOUNDED COMPLETELY OUT OF HER MIND.

SHE SAID THAT CELIA'S BROTHER HAS MOVED HIS DRUMS INTO THE KITCHEN AND PLAYS THEM MOST NIGHTS AT THREE A.M. AS AN INTIMATE, PERSONAL PROTEST AGAINST DUCKSHOOTING. I DON'T THINK THIS HELPS (EITHER THE DUCKS OR CELIA'S MUM).

I ALSO SPOKE TO YOUR FATHER ON THE PHONE TODAY. I WAS THINKING OF WATCHING A VIDEO WITH YOU THIS THURSDAY NIGHT BUT YOUR FATHER WANTS

51

TO TAKE YOU OUT TO DINNER. SO TOO BAD, I
GUESS.

    THERE'S A FROZEN PIZZA IN THE FREEZER FOR
YOUR DINNER. WHILE YOU'RE DE-FROSTING IT WHY
DON'T YOU THINK ABOUT PURPLE LIPSTICK? WRITE
DOWN ANYTHING <u>GOOD</u> THAT YOU CAN THINK OF TO
DO WITH PURPLE LIPSTICK.

LOVE FROM YOUR MUM

Mum,

There isn't one single good thing that can be said
about purple lipstick.

Love,
Elizabeth

P.S. I would much prefer to be watching a video with
you this Thursday. But don't you have your poetry club
on Thursday nights?

ELIZABETH !!!!!!

IT'S TRUE THAT I HAVE MY POETRY CLUB ON
THURSDAY NIGHTS, BUT IF I <u>DIDN'T</u> I WOULD HAVE
LOVED TO BE WATCHING A VIDEO WITH YOU, IF ONLY
YOU WEREN'T GOING OUT WITH YOUR FATHER.
    AT LEAST HE'LL FEED YOU BETTER THAN I DO.
    THERE IS SOME HAND-WASHING SOAKING IN THE

LAUNDRY BASIN AT THE MOMENT. CAN YOU SLOSH IT AROUND A BIT AND RINSE IT OUT AND HANG IT ON THE LINE BEFORE YOU GO?

WHILE YOU ARE AT SCHOOL TODAY, WHY DON'T YOU ASK YOUR FRIENDS WHAT <u>THEY</u> THINK OF <u>PURPLE</u> LIPSTICK? EXPLAIN TO YOUR FRIENDS THAT YOUR MOTHER MAY LOSE HER JOB IF SHE DOESN'T THINK OF SOMETHING GOOD ABOUT PURPLE LIPSTICK <u>VERY</u> SOON. TELL THEM THAT YOUR MOTHER'S A REALLY WONDERFUL PERSON AND IMPRESS UPON THEM WHAT A SHAME IT WOULD BE TO LOSE A JOB OVER SOMETHING AS TRIVIAL AS PURPLE LIPSTICK.

LOVE, MUM

Dear Elizabeth,

I think you're the coolest for writing letters explaining why you can't do your homework. I just don't do it, then I get busted, then I get put on detention, then I don't go to the detention cos my mum needs me at the florist shop, plus cos detention sucks. Then I don't do my homework again, then I get busted again, then I get put on detention again, then I don't go. It's a vicious cycle. It's like a washing machine with the lid jammed down.

Celia joined the circus? I can't believe it. Your friend Celia sounds like the coolest person on earth.

I read these fantastic books when I was little. There was this boy called Jimmy and the circus comes to his town, so he goes, 'Mum, can we join the circus?' so his mum goes, 'Yeah, OK, go and get your father.' And his

53

dad goes, 'Just let me wash my hands and we'll join the circus.' So they all go to the circus and luckily Jimmy finds a dog which can do magic tricks, so he gets to be a circus performer, and his dad can hammer nails and take screws out with his Swiss army pocket knife and his mum can cook big pots of stew and sew up the holes in the circus tent. (Does Celia have to cook big pots of stew or just sew up holes?)

Now that I think about it, those books really sucked.

But there was one cool bit, where this girl who's in the circus has to ride her horse to the beach to save the circus or something, so she's riding along and every now and then she just stands up on the horse's back and does a somersault in the air. And the people along the side of the street go, 'Cool' and start clapping for her with their mouths hanging open so you can see their fillings.

God, I wanted so badly for the circus to come to my town so I could do that too. I used to just stand there on my driveway watching the road in case some caravans and elephants appeared. None did, so I thought I could get a horse and teach myself to ride around standing up on it, and doing somersaults in the air. And then everyone would clap at me with their mouths hanging wide open and their tonsils in full effect.

My parents never got me a horse though. So it all came to nothing but a pile of manure.

Derek was very happy with the twig from your apple tree. He put it in one of the empty pots in my mum's florist shop so that he can grow his own tree. He says he'll send you an apple from it as soon as it's ready.

I tried to do the Smartie and M&M thing only I

closed my eyes from the beginning to the end, so that I wouldn't cheat, and then I couldn't remember which one was which. Sorry. I'm gonna buy a packet of both today and try out the experiment on everybody I know, to get you accurate results.

I'm also going to start working on your birthday present today. I've already got heaps of paper to use so I don't need to collect that. We have to read *The Merchant of Venice* and it doesn't make sense. Basically, not a single word of it makes sense. I think it would be fine if I ripped out most of the pages and used it for your birthday present. I mean, I don't think it's gonna affect the *plot* or anything. Also, I can get plenty of glue for your birthday present, because of the glue-sniffing habits of most of this school.

And I can get wax for the candle, because Derek's ear is full of it.

Sorry. That's disgusting. I'll get clean wax for you.

My birthday's in December, right next to Christmas, so it's easy to remember too, only nobody does, because it's a STUPID time for a birthday. I want a unicorn, OK? I don't want a horse any more because I've matured.

I told Derek about Celia, I hope that's OK? He wants to know if you can use your connections to get him into the circus. He's got this act worked out, where he lifts weights and whistles the soundtrack from *Titanic* the whole time. It might sound sad but it's pretty impressive when you see it.

Oh, something else has happened. My cousin Maddie is in love again. It's a relief – she was starting to get on my nerves badly. She phoned yesterday to say that a new guy has just started at her high school, and she thinks he's the hottest thing since baked potato with sour cream and mango chutney. (I know. Gross. But she goes ape for it.) He hasn't spoken a single word to her yet, she just saw him on the other side of the locker room and she swears that he winked at her. I said he probably just had something in his eye. But even if he did, she'll get him because she always does.

Good luck with your dad. Don't forget that it doesn't matter if he takes you to the poshest restaurant in the world, you will still be the coolest person there.

Love from Christina

Over one-third of the world's coffee is produced by people living in poverty. Think before you Drink.

Dear Lizzy,

HI. This is the most fantastickest thing that ever happened to me!!! The people here are the best. There's this girl called Patricia who lets me live in her caravan with her; all I have to do is polish her candelabra every now and then (she uses it as part of her act – she does a kind of elegant dinner party thing on the tightrope at the top of the tent). The circus manager is *so* nice to me. He's treating me like a kind of daughter and giving me all this advice about life and playing my cards right and stuff.

Love,
Celia

P.S. I got this stack of old postcards for free at our last venue.

Dear Ms Clarry,

So you found your best friend again. Congratulations. That's a step.

But you know what? You have the weirdest best-friend relationship we ever saw. You don't see her, you don't have her phone number, you don't even know where she is. She gets to talk to you. And you can't say a word to her.

I am really very sorry, but unless things improve soon we will have to ask you to leave our Society.

Best regards,
The Manager
Best Friends Club

Dear Christina,

I'm writing this in the backyard and it's Sunday afternoon and the apple tree thinks it's spring, and Lochie's fast asleep beside me. He's got both paws and his chin on my leg; it's the cutest thing you ever saw. Actually, it's not just cute, it's amazing. I just did a 6k run. I must smell like a rubbish truck.

I'm looking at your letter (Lochie dribbled on it, sorry. It's kind of disgusting, which it wasn't when you sent it to me) and I'm glad Maddie's practically got a new guy. But does that mean she'll get in trouble again, I mean like running away with him and that? And does it mean you don't get to see her as much? Still, it's good that you don't have to keep being her counsellor, or like her magazine problem page.

If I ever actually *talk* to Celia again I'll tell her about Derek's whistling and weight-lifting thing. She hasn't phoned me yet, just sent postcards. She probably thinks our phone's tapped or something – she's kind of paranoid like that.

I think I read those books too, the ones about the circus and the girl standing on the horse? I think it was Enid Blyton, which my mum never wanted me to read, but my dad used to send them to me for birthdays and Christmas, which made my mum just go ape. But she had to let me read them, cause they were my 'only link with my biological father'. (I heard her say that to a friend of hers on the phone one day when I was about seven.)

After that my Biological Father started coming over here for work, so I got to see him for a weekend holiday once a year anyway. Which some people might consider a better link than an Enid Blyton book but I couldn't ever completely make up my mind on that one.

Last Thursday night was the first *linking* experience of my dad's year-long stay in Australia. I just hope they're all as special and rewarding as that one was.

Ha ha.

The first thing that happened was I missed the bus. I catch the Glenorie bus, which goes right at three o'clock, basically while the bell's still ringing. I was just running along the Year 9 balcony when Mr Botherit stepped out of a classroom and stood right in my path. (Kind of like a mafia movie, where the FBI guys suddenly come out of a doorway and everything stops, dramatic like?) With most teachers, all you have to do is say, 'I catch the Glenorie bus' and they practically give you a police escort out to the bus stop.

So I say to Mr Botherit, 'I have to catch the Glenorie bus.'

And you know what he does? He says, 'Oh really?' and leans against the bag rack making his mouth twist around like he has something caught in his teeth. Maybe he had just eaten a biscuit and it was kind of packed into the gaps between his teeth, and he was trying to scoop it out with his tongue? I don't know. Your guess is as good as mine.

Anyway, he just looks at me, scratches the back of his hand and says, 'I'm wondering whether you *enjoy* our English classes?'

Give me a break.

Do I enjoy his English classes?

What are you supposed to say to that – 'Well, if you'd just liven up your delivery, throw in a few jokes and hand out occasional bags of crisps, they'd be perfect, sir'?

Strangely, I don't say that, I just say, 'Yeah, I guess.'

And he keeps on standing there, tipping his head sideways so it's practically breaking off his neck, and says, 'Do you enjoy writing essays?'

That's a tricky one because I don't think I've ever written an essay in my entire life. I usually just write a letter, explaining about how wrong it is to write essays.

So I say, 'Not really.'

And he tips his head up and down and goes, 'Hmm' and closes his eyes like I just told him something very meaningful. Like he's my psychiatrist and I just told him a dream about my childhood or whatever. You know?

So he goes, 'If you ever want to come and chat with me about your essays, do.'

I pretend to be really glad about that, and then I say again, more slowly this time, 'I have to catch the Glenorie bus' and he finally seems to click and goes 'Oh!' and lets me go.

But it's too late, of course.

I miss my bus.

If you miss the Glenorie bus, you have to wait *one* hour and take the Castle Hill bus, and then change onto the Kenthurst bus, and *then* you have to walk half an hour to get home.

Fantastic. All so I can reassure Mr Botherit that his English classes are good. I should have just recommended he go see the school counsellor if he really wants to deal with his insecurities.

So I finally get home and Dad's already there, sitting on the front verandah, trying to play with Lochie, and Lochie's looking at him like: 'Excuse me, do I know you?' and Dad's trying to get Lochie to fetch sticks, which Lochie doesn't do, because it's below his dignity, and Dad goes, 'Hey, I thought all collies fetched sticks! Guess he's not so bright as we thought, huh?'

And I feel like punching him on his stupid nose.

For one thing, Lochie is about one hundred times smarter than my dad.

I don't have time to take a shower or iron a dress, so I just throw on jeans and my white T-shirt which I know are completely wrong, and my father pretends not to notice but you can see his face go into a kind of 'whoops' expression when he sees me. But he doesn't say anything, he just drives me halfway across Sydney to this *snazzy* restaurant.

Our table has one of those white paper tablecloths which makes me think, 'Why can't they afford real tablecloths if they're so snooty?' and blue-and-white checked napkins which make me think we should be eating hamburgers. It also has a magic blue-glass bottle in the middle, which I like, with a green candle stuck in the top of it, and candle wax making a big lumpy mess down the sides of the bottle, that makes me want to scrape it all off. Plus a big chunky glass ash tray which I feel like ripping off, only I don't, because I don't have a handbag to put it in. (Also because I don't actually *want* a big glass ashtray.) (Also because I'm not actually the kind of person who rips things off from restaurants. Are you?)

So I order the chicken in orange sauce and Dad orders the spaghetti carbonara, and Dad fills up my glass with disgusting red wine, and we start having our stupid father–daughter dinner conversations.

You know, like my napkin falling off my lap and I'm reaching down to pick it up at the same time as Dad's going, 'Take a look at those picture windows, would you?' Or I've just taken a big bite of chicken which is caught on a bit of bone in my mouth and I'm trying to get it untangled with my tongue and Dad's going, 'What do you think of my tie?' and flipping it up and down in my face.

After a while we stopped talking and just ate, which is better, but embarrassing. Also I was really annoyed at the sound of my dad eating the spaghetti carbonara. He kept pushing his fork around in it, and it makes this disgusting wet, gooey noise, like people kissing or

61

rubbing their eyes. And anyway, Dad can't keep his mouth shut for more than thirty seconds. He's always saying things out of nowhere like, 'Let's go crazy, hey?'

What are you supposed to say when your father says, 'Let's go crazy?'

'All right then, Dad. Good idea. Let's'?

I'm never sure whether he says this stuff because he's got some kind of disease from living in Canada which means you can't help saying lines from American movies, or because he thinks that's the way to communicate with teenagers. I have noticed him watching me very closely after he does it, as if he's expecting me to respond in some teenager-style way. Like give him a high five or something.

If all that embarrassing stuff wasn't enough, two especially stupid things happened while we were at the restaurant.

One thing happened when we had just got our desserts. I had the chocolate mousse (which I always have) and Dad had rice pudding (which, excuse me, but why would anybody have? It's like eating cold porridge for dinner), and there was suddenly this big honking, gasping noise behind me, like someone was choking on a lobster.

I look around and this huge bald man's standing there, with a face like a pink balloon about to pop, and he's grinning at my dad and making weird noises, but it's not because he's choking on a lobster, it's because he's so excited to see my dad. He finally stops making the noises, and goes, 'ALBERT CLARRY! You old NINCOMPOOP you!'

I look back at my dad and his face has suddenly gone even pinker than the fat man's face, and he's got a spoonful of disgusting rice pudding about to enter his mouth, and it's just frozen there. One piece of rice touching his lip.

The big man doesn't seem to notice. He just shouts, 'And who's this lovely little lady?' putting his big pink hands on my shoulders. Really nice.

And Dad goes, 'This is Elizabeth.'

Then Dad looks straight at the window and starts mumbling away, 'Lovely place this, isn't it? Really nice. An old favourite of mine. Same old standards though, lovely picture windows.'

So they both talk about the picture windows for a while (if you can imagine anybody being able to stretch picture windows across a five-minute conversation) and then the man goes.

And my dad looks completely relieved. Like, he just sags down in his chair.

So, I guess he's embarrassed about me.

He didn't say, 'This is my *daughter*, Elizabeth.'

He didn't tell me who the man was.

All he did was say, 'This is Elizabeth' and look straight out the window.

Anyway, I guess I'll get over it.

The other stupid thing happened when I was drinking the froth off my cappuccino and Dad was watching me over the top of his double espresso. It was my fault. I don't even know why I said it. It just jumped out of my mouth.

I said this: 'I want to meet Veronica's son.'

Maybe that doesn't seem like a strange thing to you – asking to meet your stepbrother. Which is what he is, you know. He's the son of my father's wife, right? So you'd think it'd be a perfectly normal thing to ask for.

My father moved out when I was a baby, and he married Veronica only a few months after that, and she already had a son then – so she's been my *stepmother* and he's been my *stepbrother* for practically all my life. But I've never met either of them. I don't even know what they look like, if you can believe it. They've never come to Australia and I've never been to Canada. And for some reason my dad and I never talk about them. I used to ask when I was little, but my dad always made stupid jokes. Like I'd say, 'What's Veronica like?' and Dad'd say, 'She's just like a great big pink and purple hippopotamus!' So after a while I stopped asking. And he never talked about them, and it became kind of like a rule that we don't talk about them.

So it was breaking the rule, see?

My dad seemed to think so anyway. He just snapped out, straight away: 'He's in Canada!' like I was a complete lunatic.

I said, 'Well, maybe I could write to him?'

I don't know why I never thought of that before. I think I only thought of it now because of all the letter-writing with you.

But Dad seemed to think that was just a stupid idea. He started going on and on about how busy things are in Canada and how it would only be a disappointment to me and how you shouldn't mix your drinks without an aspirin at the ready (if you know what that was supposed to mean please let me know).

So I just gave up and slurped the rest of my cappuccino, really noisily.

I guess the dinner proved two things: one, my dad's embarrassed of me in front of his friends, two, my dad's embarrassed about me in front of his family. I

64

suppose it's no wonder, considering how I slurp my coffee.

The chicken was nice though.

Lochie is fast asleep and my leg's got pins and needles, and it's starting to get really cold out here, and I've been writing to you for too long, and you're probably sick of me.

So I have to go now. But I hope you have an excellent day today.

Love,
Elizabeth

Dear Elizabeth,

GUESS WHAT? *I know what you look like.*

You said in your last letter that you catch the Glenoric bus, which I didn't know before, but now I know, and one of my best friends catches the Glenorie bus. So I asked him if there were many people from Ashbury on it, and he says there's only two. He says there's a guy from Ashbury who sits up the front and stands up when old people get on the bus, and carries running shoes laced together around his shoulder, so that's not you. And there's a girl, so *that must be you.* He says you've got a cute face and kind of pointy ears.

IT MUST BE YOU. Is it? He also says there used to be a fairy princess girl, with long feathery blonde hair, who used to sit with you, only he hasn't seen her for ages. Is that Celia? He said he used to watch you two, and Celia always looked tiny and not-quite-there, like she was just about to float through the bus window and fly away like a kite. And you always looked like a pixie, or an elf, about to cast some magic spell over the bus. (Don't take any notice of him. That's what he's like.)

But I'm glad you've got magic powers. Maybe you can use them to help me, cos I feel like someone's put a spell on me now. Derek keeps hassling me to, you know, go all the way. I don't know how long I can keep saying no for. It'd be fine if it wasn't that *I* want it, just as much as he does, maybe even more. (Whatever you do, don't tell him that I said that.) How come I have to be in charge of stopping him? I don't get how I can keep being grown-up and saying, 'No, we have to wait', when every time he touches me I feel like I'm going crazy.

Anyway, I'm sorry to talk about my problems when you've got your own things to worry about. The dinner with your dad sounded as stupid as usual. But I thought of these things that you should remember:

1. He's only in Australia for a year. That's not exactly a lifetime, and then he'll go back to Canada and you won't have to see him any more. It probably doesn't make you feel any better but I have to listen to my father belching after dinner every night, and sometimes I wish he'd go to Canada and do his belching there. He's really proud of the way he belches – he thinks it's like an art form or something. Also, my father comes and collects me from school sometimes, in the pick-up truck, and gets out of it so everyone can see he's wearing a vest so dirty it looks like he's been rolling around in pig dung, and so ragged that you can see his fat hairy stomach through the holes, plus a pair of shorts that are falling down, and purple socks.

2. I bet your father wasn't really embarrassed – there's probably a different reason why he acted weird when that man showed up. Maybe your dad stole money from the man and he was using that exact money to pay for the chocolate mousse you were eating right then? Does your dad seem like a thief to you? There's also probably another reason why your dad doesn't want you to meet his family. Maybe they're *all* thieves? Maybe it's not a family at all, but like a criminal ring of train robbers or something? Has he ever shown any special interest in trains?

3. Maybe you could just concentrate on the food and ignore your father? Chicken in orange sauce sounds delicious. Sorry, but rice pudding is delicious too. You should order that next time. Anyway, the thing to do is to order a new and exotic thing from the menu every time you go out and then completely ignore your father and concentrate on eating. Maybe you could even bring a book along and read that while you eat, to stop him from trying to have a conversation with you? And take a Walkman too, and listen to that so you don't have to hear him eat his spaghetti.

4. If he still acts like he's embarrassed by you, you should tip your wine down the front of his shirt (making sure you get a lot of it on his tie). I actually find it hard to believe you haven't done that yet.

Lots of love,
Christina

Elizabeth,

You should be *just perfect* for advising Christina on what to do when her boyfriend wants sex.

You haven't got a clue what to say, have you?

Ever had sex, Liz? Ever even *kissed a boy?* Ever held a boy's hand, ever been asked out by a boy, ever had a boy *wink at you?*

Actually, are you sure you know what a boy is?

We are so weary of you. We are also very tired of telling you about the big white box in the kitchen where you belong.

Yours sincerely,
The Association of Teenagers

ELIZABETH !!!!

LOOK OVER HERE ON THE KITCHEN BENCH.

ABOVE THIS NOTE YOU WILL SEE A RECIPE BOOK. YOU MIGHT NOT KNOW WHAT A RECIPE BOOK IS. IT IS THE ONLY BOOK ON THE KITCHEN COUNTER UNLESS YOU HAVE PLACED ANOTHER, DIFFERENT BOOK HERE TOO.

IF YOU HAVE, REMOVE IT AT ONCE, AND YOU WILL SEE THE RECIPE BOOK.

ANOTHER CLUE IS THAT IT HAS PICTURES OF FOOD ON THE FRONT COVER. IT ALSO HAS SOME ACTUAL FOOD STUCK TO THE PAGES. THE PICTURE OF FOOD ON THE FRONT COVER IS CRANBERRY DUCK WITH SCALLOPED POTATOES. BUT I CANNOT EXPLAIN TO YOU WHAT THE ACTUAL FOOD IS BECAUSE I CANNOT IDENTIFY IT.

PLEASE PICK UP THE RECIPE BOOK AND OPEN IT
TO PAGE 124. THERE WILL BE A RECIPE THERE CALLED
'ORIENTAL CHICKEN'. CAN YOU MAKE THE <u>MARINADE</u>
FOR IT? DO YOU SEE IT? IT'S DOWN THE BOTTOM OF
THE PAGE. USE THE WHITE DISH WITH THE BLUE
FLOWERS ON THE EDGE. ALL YOU HAVE TO DO IS PUT
EACH OF THE THINGS UNDER THE HEADING
'MARINADE' IN THE WHITE DISH. THEN PUT THE
CHICKEN PIECES IN IT, AND COVER IT, AND PUT IT IN
THE FRIDGE.

THE CHICKEN PIECES ARE IN THE FRIDGE ALREADY,
SO THEY HAVE HAD EXPERIENCE BEING THERE.

I HOPE YOU HAVE FUN DOING THIS.

YOUR MUM

Mum,

The chicken is in the marinade. I had more fun than I
ever thought possible.

I'm taking Lochie to the park for a run, and then I
have to do a proper run myself. I want to do 10k today,
so I won't be back until around seven. See you then.

Love from Elizabeth

P.S. I got some new soy sauce on page 124 of your
recipe book. You can identify it because it's kind of in
the shape of a cow.

ELIZABETH !!!

THANK YOU VERY VERY MUCH FOR MAKING THE
MARINADE. IT LOOKS PERFECT. I HAVE PUT IT IN THE
OVEN AND IT WILL BE READY AROUND SEVEN-THIRTY.
HELP YOURSELF (MAKE SOME RICE TO GO WITH IT?
THERE ARE INSTRUCTIONS ON THE PACKET) AND SAVE
SOME FOR ME.
   I HAD TO GO OUT TO AN EMERGENCY MEETING OF
THE POETRY CLUB. I'LL BE BACK SOON.

LOVE,
YOUR MUM

Dear Ms Clarry,

You followed that recipe for Oriental Chicken perfectly. The
speed with which you grated that ginger, not even really sure
whether it was ginger or not! The strength in your wrist when
you squeezed the orange!
   The rice was a little gloopy but you'll soon get the knack!
Your presentation was magnificent – a sea of rice with the
chicken scattered artistically over the top! Perfect! (A glass of
cold apple juice was a really thoughtful accompaniment too.)
   Most of all, however, we are impressed by how well you
packed that dishwasher after you had finished. Moving the
knife-and-fork holder to the *far left corner* was a stroke of
genius – and the way you nestled the plastic dishes *underneath
the saucepan*!!! Heavenly! Blissful!
   One day you are sure to join our ranks!

With our Kindest Best Wishes,
Housewives of the World United

P.S. We are concerned about the Housewifeliness of your mother, though. Imagine dashing out while the Oriental Chicken was cooking! The marinade could have been ruined! How did she know whether you'd be back from your run in time to stop it burning – frizzling into nothing! Maybe you could ask her just what sort of *emergency* a poetry club has anyway?

Music that catches your soul in a fishnet – The Seaweed Savages play their latest album: Serve up the Shark Bait Platter, Hon.
Friday, February 23rd – Riverside Rathouse, Bundagai
Saturday, February 24th – Bluemoon Newmoon, Newcastle
Sunday, February 25th – Coogee All-Nighter
Monday, February 26th – Kirribilli Fun Parlour
Tuesday, February 27th – Randwick Workers Club
Wednesday, February 28th – Avoca Beach RSL
Thursday, July 29th – Terrigal Surf Lifesaving Club

HEY LIZZY. If the Seaweed Savages hadn't done so many bloody shows, there'd be room on this postcard to write to you. They played the opening number at the circus last week. The drummer bought Pat and me Orgasms all night, I was *sick as a dog*. Sorry, no more room, love, Celia.

Dear Elizabeth,

It has come to our attention that, in Celia's absence from school, you have been hanging around Daniella and Flick. It has also come to our attention that Flick brought a home-waxing kit to school today, and started waxing her legs at lunch-time, and both she and Daniella were hysterical with laughter.

You might not have found it even slightly funny, Elizabeth, but that is no excuse. The idea is to join in laughing anyway: not sit there frowning like a boring bullfrog.

Furthermore, we do not believe that you are going to make much progress in a friendship with that girl called Christina, from Brookfield. Your only hope is to offer her some excellent advice about sex.

Now, how exactly are YOU, of all people, going to manage that?

Perhaps you ought to buy a book?

Yours sincerely,
Handy Hints on How to Make Friends
(A Division of the Best Friends Club)

Click-on, click-off: The Occult comes to the Internet!
Http: www.weird.wacky.wild.demons!

Hey Lizzy,

I don't get this card either. GUESS WHAT HAPPENED TODAY? I flew. I actually flew through the air. Patricia hooked me up in these braces things, and I just went zooming up to the top of the circus tent and then spinning all over the place.

It was the most exciting, exhilarating thing that ever happened to me. I know what it's like to be a bird. The circus manager is still treating me so nice – we've started playing chess every night until three a.m. I might ask if we can play inside sometimes, cause it gets kind of cold at night, and I think I'm getting the flu! Anyway, hope you're OK, lots of love,

Celia

Dear Christina,

I don't think you should have sex if you don't want to. You should never let anyone pressure you into it. But I guess that's not the problem, is it? Cause you do want to. I don't know, maybe you just should? Or do you think that you're kind of not *ready*? I think you shouldn't do it unless you're sure that you're ready.

It's very weird that you know what I look like. Yeah, that's me, and my ears are the stupidest things in the world. How embarrassing. Too bad if I wanted to keep them a secret. Tell that friend of yours to stop watching. Though he's good at description – that's exactly what Celia's like, a fairy princess floating through the window and up into the clouds, like a paper lantern.

It's funny that he mentioned that there's also a guy from our school who catches the Glenorie bus, who always stands up for old people and has running shoes tied around his shoulders. That guy is Saxon Walker and he's never spoken a word to me in my entire life *until today*. Spooky. He actually came and sat next to me on the bus, and we talked *the whole way*. It turns out he's training for the same run as I am, so we had a lot to talk about. You know, 'marathon stories' – he told me about this famous race where one guy was *just* ahead of the other guy, but he turned around to check on him as he reached the finish line, and that tiny second meant the other guy won. I told him about a marathon in Vancouver where a man was winning by so much that he was *three miles* ahead of his nearest competitor, but he didn't realize, so he didn't stop to get a drink even though it was steaming hot and he was completely dehydrated. He ran into the stadium for the last lap, fell down, tried to stand up, and fell down again. Then he couldn't get up at all, and ambulance people rushed in, and then it was a race to save his life and he almost died.

Saxon had already heard that story actually, but he's kind of polite so he listened to the end before he told me that he knew it.

Anyway, maybe we'll even run together some time – he only lives a couple of blocks away from me. He asked about Celia too, which is nice. Most people think it's so weird that she runs away all the time, that they kind of pretend she doesn't exist any more whenever she's gone. It's not weird though, – it's just what Celia's like. She goes crazy if she doesn't have enough excitement in her life. A school counsellor once told Celia that she ran away because she was trying to find her 'adult self' which was a normal thing for adolescents to do.

Celia explained that she'd been running away since she was five years old, which is pretty young to be looking for an adult self, isn't it? So the counsellor said the reason she did it was that she felt like she had done something *wrong* in her family – maybe her parents acted in a way that made her feel *bad* – and she was trying to escape that badness. Celia asked the counsellor to please explain what she meant by 'wrong' and 'bad' because her mother had always told her that there was no thing as 'wrong/right' and 'bad/good' in Celia's life, and that every single thing that Celia chose to do was EXQUISITE.

Then the counsellor looked a bit desperate, and Celia took pity, and said, 'Actually, my father disappeared when I was about five. That could be meaningful or something, huh?' Which of course sent the counsellor crazy with happiness, jumping on the desk and saying: 'You're trying to find your daddy, aren't you, honey? That's what you're trying to do!'

Celia said she hoped she didn't find her daddy because her only memory of him was when he stopped her drinking maple syrup straight from the bottle, and she was still a bit mad about that.

After that the counsellor gave up and said, 'OK, there is no reason. You've got no excuse. So can you please just *stop*?'

The thing to do with Celia is not to try and figure her out. Although it was nice to talk to someone about her – I told Saxon about the postcards and the circus and everything. For some reason he thought it was really funny that Celia joined the circus. He couldn't stop laughing for half the bus ride.

Anyway, he's actually pretty cool. I should have talked to him before, but I kind of write off most guys in my school as total nerds.

Sorry this has to be short. I'm in Music at the moment and people are going mad with the tambourines and it's impossible to concentrate, but I wanted to write and see if you are OK, and send you this chocolate frog (I hope it hasn't melted everywhere) and say thank you very very much for the nice helpful things that you said about my dad.

Lots of love,
Elizabeth

Cruise and booze! Thai cuisine, French Champagne, jazz dancing – all in the elegant surroundings of the superb Princess Leandra!

Lizzy,

Check out the dude in the flared pants on the front of this card. Sorry it's been a while since I wrote; it didn't help going inside to play chess, I've got such a bad flu. I feel like shit – headache and sore throat and all that. But you have to keep working, you can't let the team down, so I'm not telling anyone. It also turned out to be a bit of a mistake to go inside for chess, because we went into the circus manager's own caravan, and he tried to make a move on me. He's like forty-five or something. Gross. But it's OK now because we had a really long talk about it, and I guess I was just giving the wrong signals.

Love, Celia

Mum,

I'm going to run over to Saxon Walker's place and we're going to train together. He's a guy from my school who catches my bus. He lives on Foxall Road. His mother's the local councillor so you probably met her when you did your rollerblading protest.

Love,
Elizabeth

ELIZABETH !!!

WHO IS THIS SAXON WALKER? IS HE CAROLYN WALKER'S SON?
IF HE IS, HIS MOTHER IS A DEMON FROM HELL! WHATEVER YOU DO, STAY OUT OF THEIR HOUSE. IF YOU SEE HER IN THE DISTANCE, DON'T SMILE AT HER. JUST SCOWL.

LOVE,
MUM

Mum,

It's too late. Saxon and I went for a run together and then he invited me back to his place for coffee.

His mother was quite polite for a demon from hell and she gave me a piece of carrot cake. I didn't scowl at her at all. You always said before that I should smile and say thank you to my friends' mothers. You are giving me confused and contradictory messages.

Love,
Elizabeth

ELIZABETH !

I GUESS I CAN ONLY BLAME MYSELF FOR TEACHING YOU THOSE RIDICULOUS MANNERS.

BUT IT'S NOT TOO LATE. IF YOU SEE HER AGAIN, YOU MIGHT THINK ABOUT SPITTING ON THE GROUND BEFORE HER. SAY SOMETHING CUTTING ABOUT LOCAL YOUTH AND LIBERTY AND THE IMPORTANT GROSS MOTOR SKILLS THAT CAN BE LEARNED FROM ROLLERBLADING.

I HOPE HER SON IS NOTHING LIKE HER.

LOVE, YOUR MUM

P.S. THERE IS A RECIPE FOR CURRIED SAUSAGES ON PAGE 78 OF THIS RECIPE BOOK. DO YOU THINK YOU CAN GET IT STARTED?

Mum,

Thank you very much for writing your note in enormous purple marker and sticking it right in the middle of the fridge door. By lucky chance I had invited Saxon to have coffee at our place after running today, and the brightly coloured note was impossible to miss. It was very good for him to see exactly what my mother thought of his mother.

Luckily for you, he just thought it was funny and laughed a lot.

I only just started the curried sausages 'cause I was waiting for Saxon to go home, but they're done now. (They're on top of the stove.) Just taking Lochie for a walk and I'll be back soon.

Love,
Elizabeth

Dear Elizabeth Clarry,

We feel that it is our duty to ensure that you are not getting any crazy ideas. This young man who's been talking to you on the bus? What's his name – Saxon Walker? He is simply not ever going to be interested in you.

My dear child, he is a popular boy, a cool boy, smart, funny, athletic and gorgeous. Perhaps in your imagination such a boy might be interested in you. But never in reality, Elizabeth. Never.

You are merely a running partner to him. No more.

We do not wish to offend you, only to warn you.

Best wishes,
Cold Hard Truth Association

Dear Ms Clarry,

OK, first of all, don't get your hopes up here. *This is NOT an invitation to join our Society.* Not that we think you're really hideous or anything, but you've got to be kidding! Ever seen your *ears*, Elizabeth? Ever seen the freckles on your arms?

Anyway, we're sure we don't have to explain about *that*.

We are actually writing to discuss a different (but connected) issue. See, there are certain types of boys in the world, and there are certain types of girls. For example, there are ugly girls, and there are ugly boys. It's perfectly OK for an ugly boy to ask out an ugly girl. Just as it's perfectly OK for an ordinary girl to go out with an ordinary boy. Sometimes, if necessary an ordinary girl might even choose to go out with an ugly boy, depending on how desperate she gets.

But the point is, it is *never* OK for an ordinary girl to go out with a *beautiful* boy. It would be like some kind of a distortion in the universe.

It just would not happen.

Saxon Walker is one of the most prized members of our society. He has regulation sea-blue eyes, an exquisite nose with a gorgeous little bendy bit at the end, and his cheeks have patches of pink that shift around to his ears when he's embarrassed.

He could be the son of Johnny Depp and Vanessa Paradis.

He could be Brad Pitt's cousin.

He could be a Greek god.

He could be Romeo.

Elizabeth, you are just not Juliet.

Please keep your distance from Saxon Walker, and try not to take up time that he could be spending with more appropriate young women.

With very kindest wishes,
The Society of Beautiful People (SOBP)

Dear Ms Clarry,

We hear that you have received letters from the Cold Hard Truth Association and the Society of Beautiful People? We would just like to add our support to their comments.

Only *a true teenager* could catch a guy like Saxon Walker.

A true teenager would have *waited* to see if Saxon wanted to go running again today, instead of starting off right away assuming that he would, just because you've trained together for the last few days.

A true teenager would not have got a seriously depressed look on her face when Saxon said he couldn't run today, so that he *laughed* and said, 'Don't worry, I just have to go to my judo class today. We can go running tomorrow.' (And instead of grinning like a moron at that, a true teenager would have taken the opportunity to calmly ask about Saxon's judo. A true teenager would know hilarious judo-related stories to share with Saxon.)

A true teenager would think of new and fascinating directions in conversation, instead of always coming back to the Belongil Trail Run and her new runners and her best times; and Celia's circus and Celia's headaches and Celia's circus manager – as if running and Celia were the only two things in her boring little life. (Which I suppose they are.)

A true teenager would have called out witty things from the window when Saxon got off the bus, instead of pretending to look into her school bag and then staring after him like a zombie so that when he looked around he saw her with her mouth hanging open.

And, finally, a true teenager would find some way to see Saxon when she is dressed in her nicest clothes, instead of just going running with him, so that he only ever sees her (a) in a school uniform, or (b) with her hair all sweaty and messy, her face bright pink, and her white knees sprouting from her running shorts.

You seem to have had a lot of trouble with our earlier suggestion that you get into the refrigerator. We now suggest that you take your new runners out of their shoe box and climb in there yourself. Put the lid on behind you, tightly.

Yours sincerely,
The Association of Teenagers

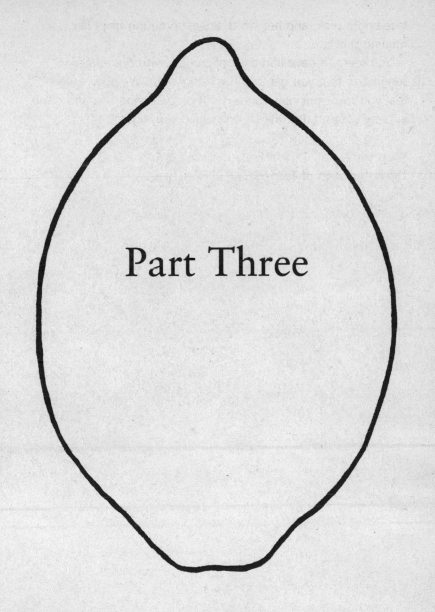

Part Three

Degas and Dance: the Art Gallery of New South Wales, 10th October–27th December

LIZZY.

Hi. Things are not exactly great at the Big Top at the moment. Ha. That's an understatement. Patricia, the girl whose caravan I'm living in? She's fighting with Miranda the juggler, and they're both fighting with Ginny the trapeze artist. Pat, Miranda and Ginny all want me to be on their side, but I think they're all acting like big losers. And the circus manager doesn't seem to be able to take no for an answer. His advice is starting to get on my nerves (so are his hairy hands). It's exhausting. I feel tired all the time, and my head hasn't stopped aching since last Tuesday. I think my glands are swelling up again too. Don't worry though, I'll be fine.

Love, Celia

Dear Christina,

You're not going to believe where I am. Actually, you've probably already guessed from my handwriting that *I'm not on solid ground*. INSTEAD, I am in something that *moves*.

Sorry. I don't even know if this will get to you. I'm going to send it to my English teacher at my school and ask him to put it in the Brookfield mail box. So I hope he does. I mean, I hope I'm not wasting my words.

Anyway, I won't tell you where I am yet, I'll start from the beginning of the story. I don't know if I mentioned it to you, but I've been getting some strange postcards from Celia at her circus. A while ago she started talking about the circus manager, and how he was being a father-figure to her, and giving her all kinds of advice. I guess she really liked that because her father isn't around. He left when Celia was about five and she can hardly even remember him. (Celia and I have been friends since pre-school and I actually remember her dad better than she does. One time Celia's family took me with them to some huge country music festival. All around people were eating KFC, but Celia's mum gave us Vita-Weat biscuits and cottage cheese. BLERK. Anyway, Celia's dad had the longest droopiest moustache you ever saw, and he spent the entire concert massaging Celia's mum's shoulders. It was so bizarre. She sat there with her legs crossed like in yoga position, and her eyes shut, and he sat behind her and massaged her shoulders with the tips of his fingers, lifting his whole hands into the air and then back onto her shoulders with a dramatic flourish, every few seconds, as if he was playing a piano concert. Celia and I giggled at them and Celia's mum had to open one eye to go mad at us.)

ANYWAY, so I guess that's why Celia liked having the circus manager treat her like a daughter. They played chess every night. (I know. Weird.) They usually played outside, but Celia was starting to get the flu so she asked if they could play inside his caravan. Which turned out to be a mistake because he started making moves on her.

So since then, I've been worried about Celia. From what she says in her postcards, her flu seems to be getting worse, and it sounds like she might have glandular fever, which she's had before and I think you can get relapses from that, and also this circus manager creep won't leave her alone.

ANYWAY, so I think I told you about this guy from my school who catches the Glenorie bus? His name's Saxon Walker and he's training for the same race as me. We've been running together for the last few days, which makes it heaps more fun. And we've been going to each other's place for a drink after we go running. He's a really nice guy, and really cute too. He laughs a *lot* at what I say, but he's also good at being serious when he has to be. And he started to get really serious when I told him about Celia's postcards. Kind of scarily serious – I was getting worried, sure, but I thought she'd probably be OK.

But *Saxon* looked like he was going to pull the emergency brake on the bus when I explained it.

'We have to rescue her,' he said, all dramatic and kind of in a rush, like we'd better get on our dragons and fly away right then.

I said, 'Um. We don't know where she is.'

Saxon thought about it for about one fifty-seventh of a second. Then he goes, 'Come on! How many circuses can there be in this country? Come over to my place and we'll try and find out.'

So I got off the bus at his stop instead of mine and he took me into his house and up the hall and into his bedroom (it's got posters of planets and stars and comets all over the walls; he said he likes astronomy), and switched on the computer on his desk.

I guess that's kind of a private school thing – a computer on your desk. I have to say right away that I don't have a computer on my desk. My mum happens to have a computer on her desk, but that's because one day she got all excited about having a home office, and stole a fax machine and a laptop from work. She never uses them except to type some of my assignments, usually at midnight the night before they're due, when she suddenly gets guilty about not having helped me to research it like the other Good Mothers do. (So if you ever happen to see one of my assignments and you think, *'Wait a minute!* She said she didn't have a computer on her desk! This looks to me *exactly* like the work of a computer!' then your next thought will have to be: 'Oh, that's right. Her mum has a stolen laptop. Please forgive me for doubting you, Elizabeth.')

SO. Within about 27 seconds Saxon's got the Internet up, and he's typing the words 'Australian Circus' into the search engine, and next thing you know there's everything you need to know about a circus right there before you. Including information on trapeze artists and clowns and where to buy the sand for the circus floor. I mean, there's not just stuff on juggling – there's instructions for how-to-juggle, and interviews with jugglers, and stories about prisoners who reformed from all their murdering and raping because they learnt how to juggle.

And there's also a list of all the circuses in Australia.

Then, this is the bit where Saxon does his detective work.

He's sitting there at his computer, leaning back in his swivel chair, frowning away, and he says, 'You know what? I just don't see Celia supporting a circus that has animals. You know what I remember? I remember when we did the frog dissection in science class? And Celia got everyone trying to revive the dead frogs with heart massage, and Hoogenboom's going, "Look, I don't mean to let you guys down, but these frogs have been in formaldehyde for the last two months", and Martin Wilson starts making frog noises with the back of his throat, like "riddup, riddup" and going, "Sir! I think I've done it! He's alive! He's alive!", and everyone's going, "It's a miracle!" and doing ritual dances to thank the gods and trying even harder to revive their own frogs and Will Stantino starts giving mouth to mouth to *his* frog, and Suzanne Reynolds sees him and throws up in the preserved snake display, and Celia gets up on her desk and demands that we call vets in to resuscitate the rest of the frogs. And anyway, Elizabeth? I just don't see Celia supporting a circus that uses animals.'

He doesn't need to tell the Science class story. He's completely right. If I'd thought about it for half a second I would have realized the same thing.

When we were four years old, Celia burst into tears when she saw the movie *Benji, not* because of what was happening in the movie, but because she thought it was terrible to make a dog act in a movie without giving it a choice whether it wanted to or not.

(I remember I was really confused about that because I hadn't worked out the whole acting/film thing – you know, I kind of thought it had really happened just in a kind of big, flat way.)

She's only written about 300 letters to the papers saying that it should be illegal to keep pet dogs unless you've got a 50-acre block of land for them to roam free on (she forgives me for having my dog Lochie because I take him for a run practically every day). She only rescues the ants on her driveway by trying to kind of herd them onto the lawn whenever her mum's about to drive into the garage.

As if she would have anything to do with a place that whipped lions and put monkeys in cages and made elephants do cartwheels on tiny little pre-school stools!

So I agreed with Saxon on that one.

Celia would not be at a circus where they have animals.

Then Saxon got this list up on the screen, of the circuses touring Australia at the moment which don't have animals.

Then *I* remembered the postcards and that the first one was from Byron Bay. So I said, 'Maybe there's somewhere that gives the tour dates and places for these circuses.'

And next thing he found *exactly that* and suddenly we had the exact name of the circus (it's called Firecrackers) and the exact place where it was scheduled to be for the next week.

And guess what?

Saxon started hyperventilating.

Well, that's what it looked like anyway. He was sitting there looking at this address for the circus, and breathing in big wheezing gasps of air, and I was shouting, 'Lean forward! Breathe into a paper bag!'

He ignored me, picked up an inhaler, and sucked it into his mouth. It turned out he's an asthmatic. I never knew that. All this time doing training with him and I never knew he had asthma.

Anyway, so he got over his asthma attack and said, 'My Auntie Robbie lives there! *Let's go!*'

Next thing, he was on his phone to his mother, his auntie, *my* mother, and the *school principal*, and he had the whole thing organized.

I never saw anything like it. He was like the bit in the movie where Tom Cruise is a lawyer and he's decided he's really going to win this case, for the sake of justice and the American *way*, and that? And it's suddenly like bang-bang-bang – grabbing files off shelves and slamming them down on the desk and punching numbers in the telephone and shaking out the phone cord dramatically, and you know, snapping out instructions to all the assistants around the desk, like: 'Get me *all* the phone records of the President of the United States for the last fifty years', and 'Get me the names of *every* client who ever ate a banana', and 'Let's get some Chinese take-away up here, on the double!'

This kind of thing to our *school principal*: 'Good afternoon? Mr Derby? Saxon Walker here. In relation to missing pupil, Celia Buckley.'

GIVE ME A BREAK.

(But *very cool*. I mean, it was kind of a turn on.)

With my mother he got me to do the talking, and then he spoke a bit himself, like a super polite private school boy, and then he asked if – get this – he asked if 'he might have his own mother phone her and assure her of my safety'!!!!!!!!!!!!!!!!

Which put *my* mother in this really difficult situation, because she happens to *hate* his mother. (His mother's a local councillor and my mum had a kind of full-on fight with her about rollerblading in the shopping mall.) (I know. Rollerblading.) (I know. In the *shopping mall*.) (I know. *My mother*.) Anyway, my mother was in this dilemma, because she hates Saxon's mother, but she had to be a good parent to me and ensure my safety.

So you know what she came up with? She *gave Saxon my FATHER'S phone number and said Saxon's mum had to call my FATHER.*

My God!

So my father must have been confused out of his mind. With some strange woman calling and saying, 'Can your daughter go away with my son?'

Actually I felt a bit sorry for him. He really wanted to do the good parent thing, but he didn't have a clue who Saxon was or who Celia was. (He probably had a bit of trouble figuring out who I was too.) But he got a bit annoying, trying *too* hard, see, getting me to explain the whole story, and talking to my mum, and Saxon, and Saxon's mother again, and even asking to call the *aunt* and talk to her.

But finally, it all worked out.

Everyone said it was fine, and Saxon phoned for train tickets.

So now you know where I am.

I'm on a train.

I'm on the way to Coffs Harbour.

And Saxon and I are going to stay with Saxon's aunt.

And we're going to rescue Celia.

But right now I'm going to stop writing because Saxon's saying we have to eat our chocolates and Pringles, and he's telling me I have to stop talking to you and start talking to him.

I'll get him to say hi to you before I stop. This is Saxon: Hi Tina. SORRY. Liz just told me you hate being called Tina. SORRY. Hi, Christina. Can you make Liz shut up and talk to me for a change instead of you? No offence, but I'm bored and starving. And she just wrote the longest letter I ever saw to you, so you've had her attention for like the entire trip, and I've just been sitting here neglected. I thought she was writing a novel or something. See you around. Saxon.

P.S. Liz just told me I had to apologize *again* for the Tina thing, but I can't really believe you're still angry.
OK, OK. Sorry, Christina.

Hi, it's me again, and I really have to go, I'm actually feeling a bit train-sick. Maybe I just need some Pringles. Oh well, wish us luck with our quest to rescue Celia.

I hope you're fine, and have a very nice day, and eat something delicious for breakfast tomorrow.

Love,
Elizabeth

Coffs Harbour at Night!

Dear Mum,

Don't worry. We didn't fall under the speeding train wheels. Saxon's auntie is really nice and she gave us cinnamon toast and hot chocolate as soon as we arrived. Her house is right on the beach so we had the cinnamon toast looking through the window at the water, and then we did our run along the beach (and we were way too slow, considering that the Trail Run is exactly *one week* away, but it was still fun). The auntie also has a lot of plants and a lot of giraffes. (She collects them.) (Not real giraffes.) So far, we haven't seen Celia but we know where the circus is and we're going there to find her tomorrow.

Love from Elizabeth

P.S. Sorry about this postcard. I know you think these are just *stupid* and *completely unfunny*, but they were on special.

Coffs Harbour in the Mist!

Dear Dad,

Just letting you know that we arrived OK, and Saxon's aunt seems nice and nothing like an axe murderer.

Have you ever been to Coffs Harbour? It's got bright colours.

Well, I've run out of room.

Lots of love,
Elizabeth

94

PRIVATE AND CONFIDENTIAL MESSAGE FOR CELIA BUCKLEY

Celia,

IF ANYBODY IS LOOKING AT YOU, PRETEND THIS IS A LETTER FROM *READER'S DIGEST* ASKING YOU TO BUY A CONDENSED VERSION OF *THE CATCHER IN THE RYE* AND MAYBE WIN FREE TULIP BUDS.

Now turn around really casually and walk away, kind of murmuring, 'Hmm. *Catcher in the Rye*, that's an OK book. Wouldn't mind a few tulips around the caravan either.'

OK.

Are you safe now?

Are you sure nobody is watching?

HI.

It's me, Elizabeth. I am here to rescue you.

I caught the train up with Saxon Walker – he was in your Geography class, you know? We're staying with his auntie and she's very very nice and she makes cinnamon toast and collects video games, giraffes and cricket memorabilia.

We have put an empty Sprite can in the tall grass next to the rubbish bin (it doesn't look suspicious, it just looks like someone threw it and missed the bin) by the gates.

You should put a reply note in there telling us the best time to rescue you.

We will hide behind the rhododendron bush after we leave this note for you, to make sure it falls into your own hands.

NOW RIP THIS LETTER INTO VERY SMALL PIECES AND *EAT THEM*. (I don't really think you should eat them cause I think that could be unhealthy especially if you have glandular fever coming; they might clog up your glands or something. But Saxon says you have to. He's going mad at me right now for saying that at all. He says you HAVE to eat it. I still don't think you sho—).

OK. Good luck, Celia.

We are with you in spirit.

Elizabeth and Saxon

Lizzy!!!!!!!!!

My God!!!!! I can't believe you're here. I never felt so weird as when I saw your handwriting wrapped around a cricket ball that was rolling towards me. (That was weird for very many reasons which I'm sure I don't need to go into.) But it's fantastic that you're here.

You know what though? You don't really need all the espionage stuff. This is just a circus, not a concentration camp. Next time you come by, why don't you just knock on my caravan door instead of hiding behind the rhododendron bush? I'll be there this arvo, around four. Can't wait to see you.

Celia

Coffs Harbour – A Bright Afternoon!

Dear Mrs Buckley,

Hi! This is just to let you know that CELIA IS FINE. We have rescued her. She is looking forward to coming back to see you and starting school again. She's got a bit of a cold at the moment, so we're going to stay with Saxon's aunt for another few days, then we'll all get the train back together. Celia says hi to you and hi to Ben. The weather is fine.

Best wishes,
Elizabeth

Coffs Harbour – A Cloudy Night!

Dear Dad,

Hello, how are you? I'm fine. Just letting you know that I'm still fine. We found the circus where my friend Celia was and we rescued her. So she's fine. Except a bit sick. I just phoned Mum and told her all about it. I hope you are well. It's pretty cool here and Saxon's auntie is still nice.
Well . . .
Hope to see you soon.

Love,
Elizabeth

Elizabeth Clarry
c/o Auntie Robbie's house,
The second house after the milkbar
with the two rusty wheelbarrows
and the broken giraffe head on the front lawn
Coffs Harbour

Dear Ms Clarry,

Those postcards to your dad and to Celia's mum were really
wonderful. Very imaginative and perfectly structured.
   No, really. You should be, like, a writer or something?

The Society of Talented and Interesting Correspondents

Dear Christina,

The rescue mission is complete. Not meaning to blow
my own trumpet or whatever, but you know what I am,
don't you? I'm a hero. A HEROINE. I'm probably the
best friend ever to live in the history of the world.

We made contact with Celia in a very clever and
tricky way. OK, this is what we did. First, we dressed
completely in green. Saxon said we had to, for
camouflage. We got Saxon's aunt to drop us off about
a block away from where the circus was stationed, and
then we slipped from tree to rubbish bin until we
reached the circus gate. We found a rhododendron
bush and hid behind that, and we were perfectly silent.
Except for when I burst out giggling. Saxon always
looked at me solemnly when I did and said he was
amazed that I could consider putting the mission into

98

jeopardy with such frivolity. That only made me worse of course.

Saxon is a big astronomy freak so he brought this mini-telescope along, so we could watch what was going on. We saw people walking along footpaths on their hands, people changing tyres, people singing together and people drinking tea around barbecues. It looked pretty cool actually and I suggested that we dump the whole rescue mission idea and just join up ourselves. Saxon looked even more amazed and said he was beginning to doubt my commitment to the task ahead.

'In a situation like this,' he said, 'it is *vital*, Elizabeth, that we operate as a team – as a *well-oiled machine*, a perfectly functioning, shiny and silver rocket-ship. Or a vending machine. One that gives change, Elizabeth, one that responds *instantly* when you touch the button that you want, *instantly* dropping a packet of barbecue crisps into the container below, and *pushing another packet forward to replace the ones that you just bought, Elizabeth!*'

I said, 'I really hate barbecue-flavoured crisps.'

He found this almost as ridiculous as my suggestion that we abandon the rescue mission, and started to demand what could possibly be wrong with me but he had to stop because *at that exact moment* we saw Celia come out of a caravan.

Amazing, I know. You don't have to tell me.

She was wearing pyjamas and a bathrobe and she had this *terrible* cough. She sounded like a sea lion.

Saxon didn't lose a single second.

He took the cricket ball that we had prepared (an old one from his aunt's collection), made sure that our note was wrapped around it carefully, and *rolled it straight across the grass towards her.* It landed right in front of her feet.

This may seem unbelievable, that somebody could aim so well, but it's true, he did.

I think he was pretty proud about it, actually. I noticed him doing a few kind of imaginary underarm pitches afterwards, looking happy and nodding at an imaginary crowd.

So, we watched Celia stare down at this ball for about half an hour. Then she picked it up, her mouth fell open (Saxon started writhing in agony then, going, 'Celia! Close your mouth! Walk away! The danger! The danger!' which made me even more hysterical) and she read it. Just standing there looking tiny in her pyjamas with her hair all messy and her bathrobe flapping in the wind.

Then she went to the shed which I think was the bathroom, and back to her caravan.

It was incredible. To see Celia again after all this time. It made tears blur my eyes.

Saxon and I went for a walk to the beach next, and I got sand in my sneakers which I still can't get out. Honestly, I've shaken my sneakers upside down at least two thousand times and *every time I do it there's still sand in them.*

When we got back to the circus, we found a note from Celia in the Sprite can where we told her to put it. She told us a Safe Time and a Safe Place where we could meet her, and we went for *another* walk along the beach until that time, and then we slipped unseen, invisible, silent (*exactly* like a Friday afternoon gym class jumping over the vaulting horse) – to the Secret Meeting Place.

And there was Celia.

It was so fantastic to see her, we just hugged each other and burst into tears, and Saxon stood beside us looking solemn for a minute and then he decided to hug us both too. I think he even had tears in his eyes.

I have to say though. Up close? Celia looked shocking. I've never seen her so wrecked. She's seriously sick I think. Her face was completely grey except for the big purple circles under her eyes, and she looked even skinnier and tinier than usual, and practically every time she opened her mouth to speak she had to cough. So she couldn't speak. One of those coughs that turn into a really deep sound, like a guard dog, so you can't really believe it's coming from a person's mouth. You know?

I also have to say that when Saxon hugged me he had great arms, and a great chest and it was hard to concentrate for a minute.

Saxon's auntie came to pick us up and she took one look at Celia and said, 'In the car. I'm taking you to the doctor.'

So that was kind of dramatic too. We went screeching off to the doctor's, Celia still in her pyjamas. Saxon's auntie was like a Speedway driver.

The doctor did a blood test but we won't get the results for a few days. He's given her some antibiotics and stuff, and said she has to go to bed for the next week. So Saxon's aunt has insisted that we all stay with her for a week, and we phoned home and it's fine, so we're all staying and it's very cool.

Although it means we're going to miss the Trail Run. Don't tell anyone but I'm a bit disappointed about that, because I've actually been training for it for about four months. Plus I came in the top twenty last year, so I had this secret dream that I would win. Anyway, I'm sure I wouldn't have won it, and Celia's far more important, so I don't really mind.

Celia seemed to kind of collapse when we got back to Auntie Robbie's. She's had a really hard time it sounds like, but she was so determined to not just quit. Now she's got Saxon's auntie taking care of her, and being shocked about all her experiences, and saying she wants to sue that circus manager for sexual harassment. It's making Celia go droopy – maybe she actually likes not being in charge for a change, and she's just lying around being pathetic. Sorry. I have to go. Saxon's auntie's asking me and Saxon to do some shopping for her. See ya.

Hi again, it's the next day and it's so so so so so so so so so so so lovely to be here at Saxon's auntie's place. Saxon even looked up his copy of *Runner's World* and he noticed that the Forest Hill Half Marathon is on in about two months. That's a really famous run and I always wanted to go in it, and Saxon says he always did too. So we're going to train for it. We've already started running again – we did our stretching together on the back verandah, and then we ran along the beach, and then we stretched together again.

At the moment, we're all sitting around in the living-room drinking hot chocolate. Saxon's auntie has this huge window looking right out across the beach which is completely deserted. It's kind of a wintry day, with a pale grey sky, and the ocean looks still and moves around lazily, and the sand is white, and there are Twix chocolate wrappers blowing in the wind. BEAUTIFUL.

Celia is resting on the couch just over there, all bundled up in blankets, surrounded by her medication and her tissues, and reading old cricket magazines.

Saxon is sitting at the table polishing his telescope and cleaning out the sand.

Saxon's aunt is playing a *very violent* video game in the other corner.

It's so nice and peaceful. The only sounds are the ocean waves, the wind, and an occasional burst of machine-gun fire.

WELL.

I guess I should finish this and send it to you, so it gets to you before I'm home.

I'm looking forward to hearing from you again. It's strange writing to you without hearing anything. It's like you and Celia have swapped places suddenly – she's here and you're far away. I hope you're not far away when I get home. I hope Derek is fine, and I hope you're fine, and I hope school's not too stupid.

See you soon, I mean write to you soon,

Elizabeth

Dearest Elizabeth,

Well now. That's more like it.

Truly, best friend behaviour.

We see you have travelled many hundreds of kilometres to save your friend from a situation of direness and distress. We see you are having long conversations with your friend again – we see you are in the same room as her! Amazing!

Congratulations!

We welcome you back into our fold.

Best Friends Club

Dear Ms Clarry,

You have probably never heard of our society. That's just as well, as we are a top-secret association and nobody ever hears of us. Not even our most prized members. We ourselves are never even entirely *certain* that we exist.

For you, however, an exception.

What a star you are! What a genius! Cross-country train journeys, camouflage and telescopes! A mission to rescue a fairy princess! Accompanied by a gallant young prince with excellent biceps! A life-saving dash to the emergency room!

We will carry you high in a velvet throne while crowds throng to catch a glimpse of you! We will bathe you in maple syrup, and crown you in silver-coated emeralds!

We will send you gossamer wings so that you can fly across the ocean on a seaweed-scented breeze!

OK?

Yours mysteriously,
The Secret and Mysterious Association of
All That Is Secret and Mysterious

Dear Elizabeth,

You and Saxon Walker make something of a team, don't you?

Together, you have rescued Celia. Together, you are spending your days running up and down the beach, sitting on the sand and squishing sea grapes at each other. Together, you are shopping for Auntie Robbie, fetching fruit and vitamin C tablets for Celia, taking turns reading books to Celia until she asks you to please shut up.

We sense many great things for you, Elizabeth! We sense

candlelit dinners, popcorn at the movies, a partner at the Year 10 formal!

We wish you the very best.

Yours,
The Young Romance Association

Dearest Elizabeth,

Excuse me while we throw up over here. Who are you trying to kid?

Try and keep in mind what Saxon looks like, would you, honey?

Cold Hard Truth Association

Richard Clarry
15–2203 Trillium Avenue
Toronto, CANADA. M5S 2H3

Dear Richard,

DON'T BE SHOCKED.

Be prepared. Maybe you want to sit down to read this? I am your stepsister.

You know Albert Clarry? Your stepfather? He happens to be my father.

Surely he has mentioned me to you?

Still, who knows. I'm very sorry if he hasn't and this is a Major Shock to you.

Anyway, has he mentioned that he used to be

married to somebody else before he met your mother? Has he mentioned that he had a *child* with that person? Well, I am that child.

I'm writing now because I'm on a train at the moment.

That might seem a strange reason to you but it's perfectly obvious to me.

Being on a train always makes me think about everything, like life and everything. I don't know why that happens to me. Maybe it's the way the train rocks? Maybe a rocking motion makes you think deep and philosophical thoughts? I wonder if that means babies are always lying in their cradles being rocked and working out the meaning of life? They probably are, you know, and it's completely wasted because they can't talk.

Anyway, I'm with two friends, and we've just been to Coffs Harbour on a kind of holiday. Now we're on our way home. Both of my friends are asleep which is why I had time to think the deep and philosophical thoughts that the train was rocking into my head.

And what I thought was this: a stepbrother and a stepsister should really be friends. Especially when I have always been an only child and always wanted a brother or a sister, and all the time there has been the possibility of a brother.

Or maybe you think I'm being stupid.

You know how your stepdad's in Australia at the moment? Well, that means I get to see him more often than usual (obviously), and we went out to dinner a few weeks ago, and I asked about you. I don't want to complain about him (I guess you know him a lot better than I do), but he always acts so strange when I ask about you. He seemed to think it was a completely MAD idea to write to you.

So I am.

I'm writing to you. I don't even know what to say. I guess I shouldn't say very much because maybe you don't want to hear from me anyhow? It's just it's been in my head, somewhere in the back of my head, ever since Dad said that it would be a mistake. I just want to find out from you if you think it's a mistake too.

So.

I hope you don't think this is crazy.

I hope you'll write back but don't worry if you don't want to.

I don't even know if I'll send this. But I think I will.

Best wishes,
Elizabeth Clarry

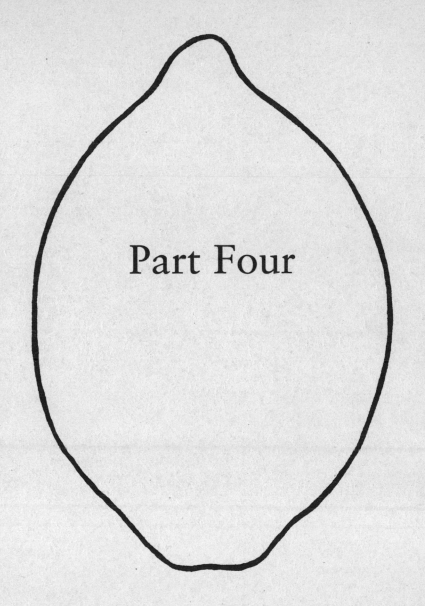

Part Four

ELIZABETH !

WELCOME BACK!
   SORRY THAT I AM NOT HERE NOW TO MEET YOU. I
HOPE CELIA'S MOTHER COLLECTED YOU ALL FROM
THE STATION OK. I HOPE YOU ARE OK.
   CALL ME AT WORK, DARLING.
   I'M VERY SORRY BUT I HAVE SOMETHING BAD TO
TELL YOU.

                                         LOVE,
                                    YOUR MUM

Elizabeth Clarry, Homeroom 27

Dear Elizabeth,

Welcome back to school – I look forward to having you
in the class again! Hope you kept up your reading
while you were away!
   I have enclosed all the letters that you received from
your pen-pal at Brookfield while you were away. I
labelled the envelopes too – letter 1, 2, etc, so you'd
know which order they arrived in. Now they're in nice
chronological order for you. Looks like he/she was
missing you!

See you in English tomorrow.

All the best,
Mr Botherit

Letter 1

Dear Elizabeth,

My God, your letter was *such a shock.* On your way to
rescue Celia??? From a *circus* in *Coffs Harbour* with a
cute guy named SAXON WALKER?????

You forgot to give me space in your letter to get over
the shock. It's the coolest. You must be the nicest, most
generous best friend in the world. I mean, OK, fair
enough, you're getting an advantage cos you're going
north with a cute guy that you like. But even so. You're
going a far far far distance just to, kind of like, *be there* for
your best friend. I really, really think you're lovely and
you should get a Best Friend Award at the next Oscars.

I have to say though, I'm kind of jealous. I know, it's
crazy. We haven't even met each other, but I still wish
you were my best friend too. (OH GOD. I SOUND
LIKE SUCH A WALRUS NOW. AND I'M EVEN
STARTING TO CRY, PRACTICALLY.) It's just that
my best friend, Maddie? I mean, she's fantastic fun to
hang around with and you know, watch MTV and eat
mango ice cream and chocolate-chip cookies. And
she's my cousin so we know just *everything* about each
other.

But now when I need her, it's kind of like she's not
really there. I mean, she's *there.* I mean, she still *exists.*

112

She's still breathing, last time I checked.

And she tries really hard to listen when I talk to her, and she gives advice and everything. But she's just. I mean. I don't know what I mean.

I have to explain. Remember I told you about that new guy at Maddie's school who she liked? Well, she decided to go out with his best friend to get him jealous, which my mum said was *morally reprehensible* and I thought so too, so I told her so, but she just said, 'A girl's gotta do what a girl's gotta do' and then did what she had to do.

So she asks out the guy's friend, and they go out a few times, and TYPICAL MADDIE, she falls for the friend. It's cos she's so obsessed by love. It means she's always kind of catching it, like a flu or something.

So she falls for the friend, who is a fucking lunatic, and get this? He talks her into sneaking out with him in the middle of this full moon night and helping him to steal his older brother's hang-glider. They take it up to the cliffs, you know the place where *normal* people go to do themselves in, but where Maddie and this guy go to have a good time.

So they get to the top of the cliff and drink like half a bottle of bourbon each to get themselves brave enough to do it. But Maddie starts chickening out and saying, 'You know, maybe we should just get a pizza and look at the stars' and this guy's saying to her in a kind of dopey voice, 'If you really love me, you will fly into the night sky with me and *touch the stars.*'

I don't know if he was being romantic or if he's so stupid he actually thought he could touch the stars. You never can tell.

Anyway, so Maddie keeps saying no, and suggesting

113

pizza toppings they could choose instead of flying to the stars, until this guy gets mad and says that if *she* won't come with him, he'll go and *fetch* her a star himself, and *that's how much he loves her* and it's *such a sad thing that she doesn't love him as much as he loves her.*

And he gets on the hang-glider all dramatic and sobbing, and goes flying off the edge of the cliff and of *course* he crashes. It's incredible he didn't die, actually. Maddie had to run all the way down to the pizza shop, and get them to call an ambulance, and helicopters had to come and rescue this stupid guy, and Maddie got to fly in the helicopter, and now the guy's in hospital in a coma, although they reckon he's going to wake up soon and he'll be fine.

ANYWAY, so Maddie is spending all her time at the hospital now trying to wake this guy up from his coma by singing lullabies to him (I tried to explain to her that *lullabies* are actually meant to put people to *sleep*, but she was too hysterical to get the point) – and when I do get to talk to her, she's just full of stories about hang-gliders and ambulances and helicopters and free ham and pineapple pizzas. The guy in the shop gave her the pizzas because he felt sorry for her.

She's not interested in my stupid complicated problem.

I just kind of wish you weren't away right now. I don't know when you're coming back, or when you'll get my letter. It's not even a problem really. It's not such a big deal. It's nothing. I'm being stupid. It's just Derek.

You know, Derek, my BOYFRIEND. And you know how he was trying to talk me into having sex and that? So I did it, just the other day. It was fine, but kind of stupid and embarrassing. Different from what I expected.

And the thing is now? For some reason I want to break up with Derek. I have all these confused thoughts in my head, like I'm angry with him. But that's stupid cos it's not his fault. I mean I said *yes*. And I only did it because I really really wanted to. I keep getting in these stupid moods where I think everything's horrible now, and ruined. Like something really important happened to me, and Derek's not taking it seriously enough. Then the next moment I think don't be stupid, it only seems like it's a big deal because people *talk* about it like it is.

Then the next moment I want to try and have sex again.

I'm just going blah blah blah and you won't even get this until you get back and I'll probably be perfectly happy by then and just about to get married to Derek or something. Good luck with Celia. I hope the rescue works well.

Love from Christina

Letter 2

Dear Elizabeth,

HELP.

What should I do?

You know in my last letter I was going on and on about how maybe I should break up with Derek and that? Well now I've got a much bigger problem. We did it again, *sex* I mean, yesterday afternoon while his parents weren't home, and this time the condom broke. How come condoms break? What's the point in them if they do that?

What I want to know is: how come there's this big anti-AIDS campaign all based on condoms, when condoms BREAK.

It ought to be illegal. People could DIE.

I'll die too, if I'm pregnant and my father finds out.

What should I do? I don't want to have an abortion, I don't want to have a baby. Should I take the morning-after pill? But how do you get the morning-after pill? Does the doctor tell you you're stupid? Is it legal to get it when you're only fifteen?

God, you won't even get this till it's too late probably. Next time I see you I'll have a little baby in a pram. Maddie'll be singing lullabies to my baby instead of to her coma boyfriend. God, my father's going to murder me.

I know it's not your fault that you're not here. Maybe I should try calling Maddie.

Love from Christina

Letter 3

Dear Elizabeth,

I took the morning-after pill. I've been throwing up all day. Mum thinks it's the new breakfast cereal she just bought, and she threw away the box. That's a real bummer cos it was delicious.

The doctor was nice, luckily, but she kept asking for

116

details about my sex life and contraception and everything. It was so embarrassing. She also seemed to think it would be a great idea if I started 'discussing these issues with my parents'.

Yeah, I can really imagine it—

'Hey, Mum, you know what happened the other day? The condom broke while Derek and I were having sex! Funny, huh?'

'Oh, bummer, Christina. Maybe you should go on the pill? Let's get Renee in here and we'll all have a chat about the best techniques.'

Or the next time Dad's giving Derek and me a lift into town:

'Oh, guess what, Dad. I took the morning-after pill the other day. Cheap condom split while we were having sex.'

'Bad luck, Christina. Maybe you should try a more expensive brand? Here, take this twenty and spoil yourself with some upmarket condoms. And while you're at it, here's a hundred bucks, Derek – why don't you take my little girl to a classy hotel and have yourself a bang-up banger of a night?'

I'm not talking to Derek now. I hate him. What if the morning-after pill doesn't work? I'll have to keep seeing Derek for the rest of my life when he comes to visit the baby. And even if he doesn't the kid'll *look* like Derek. It'll probably inherit Derek's stupid whistling talent and I'll have to listen to that whistle for ever.

I wish I had somebody to talk to. One thing I have to confess is that most of my friends at school are guys, and you just can't talk to guys about stuff like this. I don't know how that happened, I just always get on with guys. Also, girls seem to want to talk about schoolwork all the time and what marks they got and how you can use coloured pencils to shade in the margin of your history assignments in pastel pink. Guys practically never talk about school.

I know it sounds very *stupid* but sometimes I hate myself so so so so so so much. I'm so so so so so bad at schoolwork. My mum and dad say it doesn't matter, and I can run the florist shop when I'm older. I don't want to sound like a bitch, but sometimes I think I'd get bored running the florist shop and I want to do something more exciting, and get kind of successful. Then I hate myself even more for that, and I can't say that to my parents and I can't get good enough marks at school to be anything successful anyway.

I feel like throwing up again.

How come you get to have so much time off school like that? When are you coming back?

Love from Christina

Letter 4

Dear Elizabeth,

I just got your next letter from Coffs Harbour, and God, I'm so jealous – that whole hot chocolate and white sand and grey sea thing. I really wish I was there. But I'm also very proud of you. CONGRATULATIONS. You actually rescued your friend. That's fantastic – you are a fantastic best friend. The story was so exciting and you told it really well, with suspense and everything. I was hanging out to get to the end and see what happened.

I'm sorry I sent you all those hysterical letters about Derek and sex and pregnancy and everything. Now you're going to get back and read them and think I'm out of my tree. You probably won't want to ever write to me again. I'm so embarrassed. You probably won't even *have time* to read them, now you've got Celia back, and it sounds like you're practically married to that Saxon guy. Don't worry if you don't read them – it made me feel a lot better just to write to you. And I'm glad you sent me letters while you were away. They made me feel so much happier. Thanks.

That Saxon guy sounds nice by the way. He must be pretty cool if he's got an auntie who collects cricket balls and plays computer games. I liked what he wrote in your other letter too – you know how he wrote a message to me when you were on the train on the way up there? I don't forgive him for calling me Tina, of course. I never forgive anyone for that. But he still sounds nice. I hope something happens between you.

Anyway, I feel happier now. I'm not pregnant. Well, I don't think I am. What's the deal – if you get your period right away after you take the morning-after pill does that mean it WORKED and you're not pregnant, or is that a fake period and you still might be? I'm just going with the first option. And Derek and I are kind of talking to each other again, even though we're not together. I don't even get upset about that really, as long as I don't think about his body for more than a second. Don't remind me of his body, OK?

I'm doing a lot of babysitting for my mum on weekends instead of going out, so my parents can have romantic nights out. I've probably saved their marriage. And it's kind of fun watching videos and making frozen microwave meals for the kids. Although putting the kids to bed is not even this much fun: . That's a dot to show you how not fun it is making Robbo clean his teeth and wash the chewing gum out of his hair, and put on his pyjamas and get into bed. I told you he was The Devil, didn't I? Also, making Lauren go to sleep. Bloody hell. She thinks it's all a big joke, like ha ha, you're putting me in this cot and giving me this bottle and then you're going to get in too, aren't you and we'll just muck around here for a while, right? So then when you walk out of the room, she thinks, OK, you'll be back in a second to continue the game, right? So then after exactly three minutes she's worked out that it's all a TRICK and she starts this scream like a jet plane taking off.

Still, Nick's actually being helpful with the kids lately without needing to be beaten up first. And Renee lets Nick and me choose the videos and she watches us to see where I laugh so that she can laugh at the right place. Plus she does the washing-up after the microwave meals.

And I thought of a career too. I heard about this thing called Management Consultancy and you can get rich, and all you've got to do is tell people how to get stuff done more quickly. You don't even have to be smart or anything. And I reckon I would be so excellent at that. I mean, all the time, all around me, I see how slowly everyone does everything. E.g. The postman just kind of strolls along the footpath and then flicks through his letters before he puts them in the boxes; the woman at the fish and chip shop stares out of the window for a while before she thinks about putting the potatoes in the oil.

And you should hear how long my Maths teacher takes to tell us what we're meant to do for homework. This is an example: 'Probably the – ah – best – er – thing (cough) – at this stage of the game – ah – is – for you to try your – ah – hand, at the, what shall we say? Shall we say the – er – 7th and 8th – ah, no – yes, I think, I would say we should – er – discuss – yes, shall we say the 6th? Not the 6th! Crazy me! Wait on! Sit still! The 7th – yes, ah, er, the 7th unit in chapter, what chapter is that in? What chapter are we in? Ah. Yes, chapter 13. So let me ah er ah er ah er go over that one more time . . .'

And that's the biggest waste of time of them all because not one single person in my class does Maths homework.

Anyway, it would be so easy to make these kind of people do stuff more quickly. E.g. You could say to them: 'HURRY UP.'

You could hire a team of huge men with voices that sound like they need to clear their throat, plus a team of scraggy little women with shrieking voices (my History teacher would be an example), and you could get these people just to run around behind the slow people, shouting, 'GO FASTER, HURRY UP, TOO SLOW.'

You could get some weight-lifting muscle-man leaning over my Maths teacher's shoulder, going, 'Get a bloody move on, you moron.'

I shouldn't have talked about weight-lifting. Now I'm thinking about Derek's body again.

But anyway, so I'm not having a baby and I've got a career sorted out, so I feel much better.

121

Oh and guess what? Maddie's coma-boy woke up. But guess what else? Maddie's already in love with somebody else – it's that first guy who she's been in love with all along. You know she started going out with coma-boy so she could make his friend jealous? So the friend came to the hospital to visit coma-boy while Maddie was there, singing lullabies for him. And the friend tells Maddie she's got the most beautiful lullaby voice he ever encountered. So coma-boy wakes up, and Maddie tells him she's leaving him for his best friend. Nice. It's amazing he didn't fall back into a coma. She hadn't even got the best friend yet, but that's her style: she just announces she's going to get someone and she does. I guess him liking her singing voice is a pretty big start because man, she's got the worst singing voice.

OK, I have to go. I almost said 'see you soon' just then, but I guess I won't. We should meet some time though, don't you reckon?

Love from Christina

Dear Christina,

I just finished reading all the letters that you sent while I was away. My English teacher collected them for me and labelled them and everything. DON'T WORRY. He didn't read them. The envelopes were sealed up properly. I checked.

I am so so so so so so so so so so so so so so so so sorry that I wasn't here when you were going through all that stuff.

I feel really guilty. I hate myself. I'm so glad that you feel better now, and you're not pregnant and everything. And you've got a career. Management Consultant. That sounds cool.

But you and Derek broke up and I can't believe it. You sound like you're coping well, but I bet you're really sad. Do you think there's any chance of getting back together? Are you OK?

Getting your letters was the best thing that happened to me all day. I waited till I got home to read them, so that I'd have something to look forward to. Then I read them lying on my bed and eating a raspberry Pop-Tart. I hope that's all right.

Something happened to me but I don't really feel like talking about it. For one thing I'm always talking about myself instead of about you, and now I feel guilty and I hate myself because I wasn't here when you needed me.

I was rescuing Celia.

And maybe I should have left her right where she was.

Anyway, I think I might go watch TV. I'm sorry I don't feel like writing any more. I feel kind of drained of energy – like I've hit the wall. (That's marathon talk – it happens when your muscles can't take in any more oxygen and you feel like you're about to die.)

But I got you this charm at the shops today, to try and make you feel better about stuff. I've got a feeling you're not the type of person to have a charm bracelet but this one's kind of funny, it's not like a star or a princess or anything. It's got a really cute face, don't you reckon?

Also here's some raspberry that I accidentally got on

123

the letter (eating my third raspberry Pop-Tart today), but it's kind of pretty:

Anyway.

Write soon,

Love from Elizabeth

Dear Elizabeth,

What happened to you?

Tell me.

Don't be stupid – you do *not* always talk about yourself, you walrus-head. I always talk about myself. You're a fantastic letter-listener and you sent me a charm that I *love* and I put it on a piece of string around my neck, and it's very very cute. THANK YOU. And you always say the right thing in your letters and you always guess how I'm feeling.

Like about Derek. It's true that I'm just kind of pretending not to mind that we've broken up. I don't have any idea if we're going to get back together again. Sometimes I think there's no way possible, and it's like we're strangers who never spoke to each other before. But other times I think for sure we will, and we know everything about each other, and it's just stupid that we're not together now.

Sometimes I think, well I wasn't planning on *marrying* him anyway, so maybe I should just try meeting someone new, and it even seems kind of exciting. Other times I see him coming towards me across the art room, and I forget we've broken up and I think he's going to give me a big gorilla hug

124

because he's got that weird smile on his face that he gets when he's going to give me a big gorilla hug. But then he walks straight past me, and he's just smiling in his gorilla hug way at the 'WASH ALL PAINT PALETTES BEFORE YOU LEAVE' sign on the wall.

Anyway, I want to send this right away so you get it today, because I'm worried about you. What happened to you? How come you said you should have left Celia where she was? Did Celia do something bad to you?

But if you really don't feel like talking about it, that's fine, you don't have to. But maybe it'll make you feel better. And DEFINITELY DON'T keep quiet about it just because you feel guilty.

You haven't got anything to feel guilty about.

Write soon.

Love from Christina

Dear Christina,

Your letter made me cry. Because you're the nicest person in the world I think, maybe.

I'm not really doing anything. I'm just lying on my bed and it's the middle of the night and I haven't gone to sleep yet. The blind is hanging crookedly and letting moon shadows fall all over the wall.

I can't do anything except lie on my back, and think all around my empty room, listening to nothing. I would listen to music but it might wake my mum up.

I had such a long, long, long shower. You would go mad at me if you were one of those consultant people that you're going to turn into. I was so slow and wasteful. I twisted the shower around so it sprayed against the wall and I just leaned there with the water making patterns all around me and sliding down the tiles.

The last few days I've been feeling like I can hear people crying everywhere. Behind the shower water I could hear a sound like someone just sobbing and sobbing. I hear it behind everything. Behind the noise of the school bell ringing, or the noise of everyone talking in the canteen, or even the noise of a teacher shouting at someone. Behind my music, behind lawnmowers, behind the television, all I can hear is a sound like somebody crying.

Sometimes, behind the shower and behind the music, and behind the crying, I hear the telephone ringing too.

Sometimes I am so sure that the phone is ringing I turn off the shower and stand there naked listening.

It's never the telephone. The telephone never rings.

Do you think there's something wrong with me?

Love from
Elizabeth

P.S. You asked what happened to me, and I don't mind telling you, that's fine. It was nothing really. Nothing important like thinking I'm pregnant or breaking up with a boyfriend. It was just something small and stupid. I'm too embarrassed to tell you because it's small and stupid. Maybe tomorrow.

126

Dearest, dearest Elizabeth,

You are crazy.

Not because you're hearing sounds and everything, I've got a feeling that's normal. I asked my mother about it and she said she gets exactly the same thing. (I didn't tell her it was you, I just asked her like *hypothetically*). That's the crying sound – my mum gets that too. That's probably because she's got hypersensitive baby radar switched on, and she's hearing all the babies in the world whenever they cry. Maybe you've got the same thing? Maybe you're hearing LAUREN cry whenever you hear a crying sound? She's crying a lot lately because she's getting a new tooth, so probably that's it.

But the telephone ringing sound, everybody gets. I do for sure. The whole time I'm working in the florist shop I'm picking up the phone and there's nobody there. It turns out it was just a bird singing or someone wheeling a rubbish bin round the back of the shop.

It's because I keep expecting the phone to ring, because I think Derek's going to call.

But he hasn't called.

Anyway, you're still crazy. Because it's crazy to be too embarrassed to tell me something that has got you upset. God, Derek's an idiot who can't stop talking about his muscles and whistling stupid shit – how can it be the biggest thing in the world that we broke up? It's not. And it's *not* important that I thought I was pregnant. It would be important if I *was* pregnant, but I'm not. Even if I was, that wouldn't make things that happened to you stupid. Anything that makes you feel unhappy is important and I really want to know, and see if I can help you.

Please stop being crazy.

Lots of love,
Christina

Dear Christina,

OK, I'll tell you what happened.

But trust me, it's just stupid.

Well, Celia and Saxon and I got the train back from Coffs Harbour and it was really cool. We were all getting on so well, and sometimes we read books or magazines, and sometimes we played games like Hangman or Boxes, and sometimes we just talked. We had great conversations, everyone saying funny things and everyone laughing. One time we decided to get food, and Saxon and I *insisted* that Celia stay sitting while we went and got it for her. Because she's still not very well, see. We were looking after her, and both of us making sure she was warm and drinking plenty of water and everything.

Saxon and I walked all along the train, right up to the other end looking for somewhere to buy food. He checked that I was OK in the scary bits between the carriages, when the train's shaking and it feels like the metal bits are going to collapse beneath your feet. That's how I feel between carriages anyway. And Saxon held open the door for me, and even took my hand sometimes to make sure I was all right.

We got right up to the other end of the train and

there was no cafeteria carriage. We had to turn around and go all the way back. We went past Celia really quietly so she wouldn't know we'd gone in the wrong direction, and she didn't see us because she was leaning her cheek against the window and watching the banana plantations go by. It turned out that the cafeteria carriage was the *very next one down*. Like just one carriage in the other direction. For some reason Saxon and I thought this was the most hilarious thing ever to happen. We just stood there wobbling in the cafeteria carriage, laughing and laughing and laughing.

The guy behind the counter waited patiently, and the train bumped a bit, and we kind of fell against each other, and we were rocking, hugging each other, and laughing, and practically crying. No I think actually crying. That's how much we were laughing.

Then we bought Cokes and sausage rolls and crisps (which cost like a million dollars on trains – did you know trains rip you off just like they do at movies with popcorn?) and we took them back to Celia, and we were kind of hiccuping laughter, and our stomachs hurt from laughing.

I think when the train pulled in to Central Station, and Celia's mother was standing there holding an enormous sunflower in her hand, I actually felt happier than ever in my life before. My best friend was practically flying off the train to see her mum, and Saxon and I were standing back and looking at each other, kind of like, 'Isn't that nice?' and feeling proud of ourselves, and carrying Celia's stuff between us.

Then Celia's mum gave Saxon and me a big hug too and said, 'Thank you for bringing my little shooting star home with you', and we all cried.

129

Celia's mum dropped me off at my place first, and we all said, 'See you on the bus tomorrow' and I just felt like everything had changed colour in the world. Like this really special feeling of being sun-burnt and sandy would stay forever. Like from now on everything would be the three of us in the basket of a hot-air balloon, floating around the clouds together.

I went inside my house and straight away the good feeling went bad.

Straight away I had this sensation like something was wrong.

My mum wasn't there, but there was a note on the fridge from her, which said, 'Call me at work. I have something bad to tell you.'

So I called her.

And then I realized what was wrong in the house.

My dog wasn't there.

It was because he was dead.

I never thought that could happen. I mean, seriously, I never once imagined that Lochie could just *die*. It was because he got hit by a car. My God, I don't know why I never thought that might happen considering that we live on a really busy road, and bloody semi-trailers go past our place all the time. And Lochie's favourite hobby was escorting them up the road.

I just thought he was being polite, you know?

It happened a couple of days before I got back, my mum told me, and whoever did it didn't even stop. Mum found Lochie when she came home from work that day – he'd crawled on his stomach all the way down the street and ripped his stomach open, and left a trail of blood, and he was just lying in our front yard.

130

I know people's dogs die all the time, and it's not like a grandma dying or anything. I mean, you're supposed to just go, 'Oh well, at least he didn't get old and sick and arthritic, at least he died when he was still chasing semis down the street.'

But I couldn't make anything work that night. I couldn't make my head work or my arms and legs work. I just went dead all over.

Mum came home and made me chicken noodle soup and put me to bed like a little girl.

And the only thing keeping me going was this: I was thinking, 'I'll tell Saxon and Celia tomorrow.' Just over and over. 'I'll tell Saxon and Celia as soon as I get on the bus.'

So the next morning, I got on the bus and that had turned into a kind of chant in my head, 'I'll tell Saxon and Celia' – and somehow that was going to make everything OK.

They got on at their stop and I'd saved a seat for them behind me.

So I turned around and said hello, and I was thinking in my head, 'don't cry, don't cry, don't cry,' and I told them.

They were nice, of course, in a kind of friendly way. Like, 'Oh no, that's terrible.' But it wasn't going how I imagined. They were looking at each other and going, 'God, how awful' and it just wasn't going to cure me.

Then for some reason I *wanted* to cry, like my whole head was full of tears, and I wanted to cry and cry, and for them to hug me, and everyone to stare. But I couldn't cry. It was like I wanted it too much and that was blocking the tears.

Celia and Saxon did their 'Oh, Elizabeth, that's so awful' thing for a few minutes. And then Saxon says this: 'Yeah, I know how you feel, Elizabeth. One of the horses on my dad's farm had to get shot last year because of an infection. I was just gutted by it. I loved that horse. But we've still got other horses at the farm and that makes me feel better. Maybe you should think about getting another dog?'

And Celia says, 'Well, maybe, but maybe it wasn't fair having a dog in suburbia anyway? It's not really where dogs belong.'

And Saxon says, 'That reminds me, Celia. I want to ask you to come and stay on our farm with me some weekend soon. My parents think it might be good for you to get some country air.'

And Celia says, 'Sure.'

And they start talking about the farm, and horse-riding, and sheep and cow manure and leeches.

And they never say another word about my dog.

And Saxon never asks me to go to the farm too. Just Celia.

And when we're getting off the bus, I say to Saxon, 'You want to come running with me tonight?'

Saxon says he thinks his knee's playing up and he doesn't think he wants to go in the Forest Hill Half Marathon any more, because he thinks we missed too much training up in Coffs Harbour, and plus he has to catch up on his schoolwork (give me a break).

Then, as we're going into school, Celia whispers to me, 'He wants me to see a movie with him tonight. Cool, huh?'

So, that's what happened.

Stupid, isn't it.

132

I should go. I have to start making dinner before my mum gets back from work.

Love from
Elizabeth

Dear Elizabeth,

You know, you can take the whole best friend thing too far.

Celia would have been OK without you rescuing her. She's always OK.

But back here, Christina needed you, and you weren't here for her.

And Lochie needed you. He was probably lying there in your front garden crying for you, wondering where you were, hour after hour.

And where were you?

Try and think about who your *real* friends are in the future, huh?

Sincerely,
Best Friends Club

Dear Elizabeth,

Just letting you know we've withdrawn your name from our mailing list.

There is nothing remotely secret or mysterious about you. You're just a dumb teenager who got some crazy ideas about herself.

As far as you are concerned, we no longer exist.

As far as we are concerned, you no longer exist.
Please destroy this letter.

Yours contemptuously,
The Secret and Mysterious Association of
All That Is Secret and Mysterious

Dear Elizabeth,

There is nothing romantic about you.

We think that a tiny part of you was actually happy that your dog had died.

Because you thought that would make Saxon Walker go all googly over you, didn't you? You actually thought he might take you in his arms and hug you, and you thought he might cry with you, for you, and for your dog, and you thought he might ask you out to try and cheer you up.

And you thought he might hug you again when you went out, didn't you, and you thought you might look beautiful with tears on your lashes and your eyes glinting, and a terrible, beautiful sadness on your face.

And you thought he would be swept away by you, and that he would kiss the tears from around your eyes, and kiss your forehead to comfort you, and hold your elbows gently, and kiss the tears on your cheeks, and then his mouth would find your mouth and kiss you over and over.

You thought all that, didn't you, and you were glad that your dog had died, weren't you?

You ought to be ashamed of yourself.

We want nothing to do with you.

The Young Romance Association

Dear Elizabeth,

We told you so.

Cold Hard Truth Association

Wallpaper your bedroom in black, Elizabeth;
Close the curtains, pull down the blind, turn off your light,
and
Turn up your stereo loud, Elizabeth
louder,
louder,
louder,
We see no point in you, Elizabeth,
We think you ought to be dead.
We don't see why you bother existing at all.

Sincerely,
The Association of Teenagers

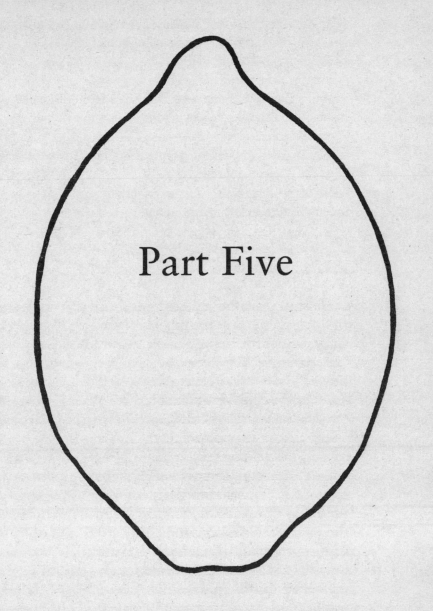

Part Five

Dear Elizabeth,

I'm incredibly sorry about your dog dying.

From
A stranger

Dear Elizabeth,

Look, we've just had word that you found an anonymous note in your bag when you got home from school today. Could you confirm this for us? Give us a sign by opening your window at midnight tonight and mooing at the stars.

We don't want to raise your hopes or anything, but anonymous notes are really the essence of who we are. Anonymous notes chime the bells in haunted towers, curl the creeping vines on gateways, rust the locks, toss the shadows, weave the spiderwebs, breathe the nightmares! Anonymous notes are right where it's at!

We are therefore pleased to make a provisional offer of membership in our society. Our offer is only provisional because we don't trust you.

Yours single-eyebrow-raisedly,
The Secret and Mysterious Association of
All That Is Secret and Mysterious

Elizabeth,

That anonymous note you got today? I bet it was from some old woman who overheard you telling your friends about your dead dog.
After she wrote the note she dropped dead too.

Best wishes,
Cold Hard Truth Association

Dear Elizabeth,

Another thing.
You're a waste of space.
How come you don't just drop dead yourself?

All the best,
Cold Hard Truth Association

Dear Elizabeth,

Your hair looks really shocking today. What's with that weird fringe curling in two opposite directions like curtains opening on a stage? You want to make a kind of centrepiece of your forehead, Liz? Is that the effect you're trying for? How about throwing in a spotlight for the zit on your forehead, huh?
I can't believe you went to school looking like that.
Maybe you should give us a call some time?

The Director
International Department of Hairpieces, Toupees and Wigs

140

Dear Elizabeth,

No! Of course you shouldn't do any homework! Are you out of
your mind? What have you got anyway? Maths! NEVER do
Maths homework. Nobody checks! And Mr Valcino writes up
solutions to the tricky ones on the board at the start of the
lesson! So it's a WASTE OF TIME to try and work them out
yourself.

You weren't actually thinking of starting work on that Music
assignment were you?! Ha!! Excuse us a minute while we
chortle hysterically. Have you got this far without figuring out
what Term Assignments mean? They're just JOKING when they
say work on it all term! What they mean is stay up all night the
night before it's due! You crazy kid, you!

Good God, child, you have absolutely NO homework.

Fond regards,
The Society of People Who Are
Definitely Going to Fail High School
(and Most Probably Life as Well!)

Dear Elizabeth,

Oh, good idea. No, look don't bother doing any training today.
It's FAR better to lie on a couch eating an entire packet of Tim
Tams and drinking a bottle of Coke than to attempt to rekindle
a fading, failing, never-got-off-the-ground career as a distance
runner! Think about how much time you lost when you had that
flu! Think about how much more time you lost rescuing the
delightfully grateful Celia. Think about how stupid it is running
alone now that Saxon's decided to drop out.

141

Watch TV instead! Watch *Wheel of Fortune!* Choose a participant and shout encouragement from the couch. 'Go Mary-Anne. Come on, Mary-Anne.' Guess what prize they're going to pick! You can get the same high from watching the wheel spin just past Bankrupt as you can from running 20ks! And you won't be nearly so sweaty!

Yours ever,
The Society of High School Runners Who Aren't Very Good at Long-Distance Running But Would Be if They Just Trained

ELIZABETH !!!

OVER HERE! ON THE FRIDGE!
THERE'S A SPECIAL TREAT FOR YOU INSIDE THIS FRIDGE. JUST BEHIND THIS DOOR. JUST ON THE TOP SHELF.
IT'S A STRAWBERRY MANGO! AND THEY'RE NOT EVEN IN SEASON!
YOU CAN TAKE IT TO SCHOOL WITH YOU IF YOU LIKE. I'M NOT SURE HOW YOU'LL EAT IT THOUGH.
THOSE THINGS CAN BE REALLY MESSY.
AS ANOTHER TREAT I HAVE DECIDED TO STAY HOME TONIGHT INSTEAD OF GOING TO POETRY CLUB.
THE POETRY CLUB WILL COME HERE.
IF YOU FELT LIKE MAKING A CAKE OR A SLICE FOR THEM THIS AFTERNOON, PLEASE FEEL FREE. IN FACT, I HAVE LEFT A RECIPE FOR A CHERRY AND APRICOT SLICE ON THE BENCH, AND IN THE CUPBOARD YOU WILL FIND SPECIALLY PURCHASED

CHERRIES, APRICOTS, WALNUTS AND CONDENSED
MILK! JUST AS THE RECIPE REQUIRES!
  BUT ONLY IF YOU FEEL UP TO IT.

LOTS OF LOVE,
YOUR MUM

Dear Elizabeth,

My God. I cannot believe that you actually thought that
was too unimportant to tell me about. Your dog died
and the boy you were in love with asked your best
friend out. And that's just nothing. Good Christ,
Elizabeth Clarry.
  Hello? Are you there?
  Look, one tiny aspect of that story would have been
serious enough. Even if your dog had just sprained his
little paw. Even if Celia had done a sexy eyebrow thing
at Saxon. As it is – I can't believe it. You're so incredibly
brave. If those things had happened to me, I'd have
been buying myself a freezer full of Ben and Jerry's and
moving into the treehouse out the back.
  This is so serious that I'm skipping Commerce to
write to you and that is one major sacrifice. Do you
realize we're doing Skills for Product Differentiation at
the Supermarket today? How am I ever going to be able
to choose between Kraft Slices and Coon Mature
Cheddar when I'm a housewife with a trolley full of
kids at Franklins? You want to tell me that?
  No but seriously, Elizabeth, that was the saddest story
I ever read. You are so brave. Your dog dying. Jesus, I

143

cried myself to sleep for about three years when Josie (my lab–kelpie cross) died. Here is a very top-secret secret, and swear to me you won't tell anybody, but I was MUCH more upset about my dog dying than about my grandma dying. You remember I told you that my sister Renee saved my grandma's life by calling an ambulance last year? Well, she only saved it for another month because then she had a massive heart attack and died anyway.

So I was upset and all, and cried at the funeral, and it was awful around the house (although we had a lot of butterfly cupcakes, which everyone seemed to bring after the funeral), and my mum went really peculiar. But really, my grandma was always losing her temper and shouting at Robbo, which only makes him worse, or going mad on my mum for the kind of gardening gloves she chooses, or telling me that I'm getting nice and fat. Thanks Grandma. Whereas my dog never once shouted at Robbo or complained about Mum's gardening gloves or told me that I'm fat. My dog was perfectly happy with everything about our family and just sat around smiling.

The fact is, my dog was nicer than my grandma.

God, I shouldn't have told you that. You're going to think I'm a cold and callous witch.

Oh well, too late.

Also, it's so sad about Saxon. It sounded like it was really going to work out, and he seemed pretty cool. And then Celia just being excited about Saxon asking her out. God, Elizabeth, that must have been like losing Celia again. I guess she didn't realize anything about how you felt about Saxon, or else she wouldn't have been so insensitive. (Still, I don't want to say anything because I know she's a good friend, but seriously, what was she thinking?)

So what's happening now with you and Celia and Saxon? Are you hanging out together or is it unbearable? Is Celia coming to school or is she still sick? And does everyone think she's a goddess or something because she joined the circus?

You know, what I was thinking is that if you want to TALK about anything we could do it out loud. I mean, in the same room. Using words and that. We could meet whenever you want.

Make sure you tell me if you're upset about anything in the future, OK, and try not to be too sad. I got you a charm to cheer you up – sorry to copy your idea, but it was such a cool idea. It's a unicorn flying, if you didn't notice, because I know you like flying. I know unicorns aren't supposed to fly but I think wings are a very smart addition and I for one would like to congratulate the manufacturer for thinking of it.

I like unicorns too. So the unicorn with wings is a present from me to you.

Lots of love,
Christina

Dear Christina,

Thank you very very much for your nice letter and the BEAUTIFUL charm. How come your letters keep making me cry these days? I wish I'd told you about Lochie and Saxon earlier, because you always make me feel better.

Thanks for skipping Commerce to write to me too. I'm skipping Liturgical Dance right now to write to you, but it's not really a fair exchange. I mean, I can't think of a single point in my life where I'm going to be in crisis because of not knowing how to dance liturgically. Whereas you are now going to be in crisis every time you go to the supermarket for the rest of your life.

I just read your letter again and I noticed that you haven't said a single thing about yourself. It's all about me. Now I feel selfish. You're a very nice person, you know? So, what's happening with you, and what about Derek? And what about your cousin, Maddie? And what about your brothers and sisters? Has your baby sister learnt how to walk without tipping sideways yet?

So. Anyway. I still don't feel exactly ecstatic but I'm not so miserable any more. It was stupid of me to think Saxon would be interested in me – he's way above my level. He's like gorgeous or something. Celia's coming to school but she's still got this cough that makes people stop halfway through words and stare at her, and makes teachers panic, like, 'Uh oh, what does it say in the teacher's manual about students dropping dead in the middle of Maths again?' Saxon spends most of his time looking from Celia to any passers-by and back again, like he's a scientist who's just seen that the end of the world is coming and nobody's taking any notice. He's always trying to make sure she's warm enough and bringing oranges and kiwifruit to school for the vitamin C. Celia just coughs at him and giggles.

Saxon has stopped going to his own classes so he can

sit by Celia in all her classes, with his mobile on hand, in case she needs medical supplies. He also supports anything she says which is irritating since he's not in most of her classes and doesn't have a clue what he's talking about.

I hardly ever see Celia outside school now, because she can't go out – the doctor says she overdid it when she got back from Coffs, and 'gallivanted around' when she wasn't ready for it yet. Now she's supposed to sleep all the time, or at least sit around not getting over-excited. This would normally be literally impossible for Celia, because she lives on excitement. But now she doesn't even seem to care. She's just listless. When I visit her she drags her quilt around the room and watches MTV. So I don't visit her very much any more.

I think I should talk to her or something. Maybe even write her a letter? But what would I say? Excuse me, but I liked your boyfriend before you did. Please give him back.

Anyway, it's more than that – it's like she's disappearing. You were so right when you said it was like I'd lost her again. How could she not have noticed that I liked Saxon? How could she not realize how upset I was? The Celia I USED to know would have noticed. I think. Maybe something's seriously wrong with her. Maybe I should write a letter that just says: 'Celia? Celia? Hello? Where are you?'

It'd be weird writing a letter to Celia. I've known her so long. It'd be like writing a letter to myself.

She should just know.

My mum's trying to be nice to me because she knows I'm upset. Like, for example, she invited the poetry

147

club to our house last night, instead of going out and leaving me alone. Big step, Mum. I made her a cherry and apricot slice for the club, and you know what, I'm going to put a piece of it in this letter, because I brought some to school with me for lunch. You will notice that it's the best cherry and apricot slice you ever tasted, probably.

I thought I would just watch TV while the poetry club was there but Mum seemed to think that part of the cheering-me-up strategy was getting me to sit in on the meeting. It turned out that what poetry clubs do each week is make two of the members the leaders. One leader chooses a favourite poem and reads it out, and then they discuss it. The other leader brings a poem written by HERSELF and reads that out and then they all talk about how wonderful and talented that person is.

Remind me never to join a poetry club.

This week it was Mrs Lorenzo's turn to choose a favourite poem and she chose Walt Whitman, and he's written the longest poem in living history. It starts off something like, 'I celebrate myself, and sing myself' and then it goes on for about three thousand pages celebrating and singing itself. I mean, puhlease. The others had to tell Mrs Lorenzo that they'd heard enough eventually. They said they would read the rest on their own but Mr Rotherham left his copy on the floor under his chair so HE'S not going to read the rest on his own. Then they talked about it for a while and they were especially excited about this one line that goes, 'Have you felt so proud to get at the meaning of poems?' Because they all feel so proud to be getting at the meaning of poems every Thursday night over carrot cake and cherry and apricot slice.

My dad called in the middle of Mrs Lorenzo's reading to find out if I wanted to go out with him some time soon, and afterwards Mum kept saying to the others, 'Well, this is it, see? It's plain inconsiderateness.'

I don't understand how Dad was supposed to know she was having a poetry reading that night, so I don't know what's so inconsiderate about it.

It was Mrs Koutchavelis's turn to read out her OWN poem and luckily it was short. It went something like this: 'I am the answer. I am the question. Ask me my question? Question my answer! Answer my question! I blow, I breathe, I bubble.' I think she made it up while Mrs Lorenzo was reading out Walt Whitman.

At the end of the poetry readings Mum asked everyone to please think up a slogan for raspberry-flavoured cat food.

Well, I'd better go. I'm so glad I met you through this letter-writing and yeah, I think we should meet in human living form one day too.

Lots of love,
Elizabeth

P.S. I guess you were only joking when you said you couldn't tell which was the better out of Coon Mature Cheddar and Kraft slices? I'm not even going to bother with the correct answer, it's *so* obvious.

P.P.S. Do you seriously not know? Maybe you shouldn't skip any more Commerce classes?

P.P.P.S. I don't think you're a witch for being more upset about your dog dying than your grandma. Sometimes dogs are nicer than people. That's not your fault. And it would be DISHONEST to be upset about someone who you never really liked.

P.P.P.P.S. Although I wouldn't mention it to your mum.

Dear Elizabeth,

I hope you're not getting happy are you? Not getting a little zip of good cheer as you run along this embankment? You've got no reason to be happy, you realize that, don't you? Say you were ever to meet that Christina? She'd drop you like a bowling ball. She'd be out of there before you could say ilio-tibial band syndrome. (A common condition which can be caused by over-training, Elizabeth, in case you'd forgotten, and one that you sure aren't ever going to get since you practically never even TRAIN, let alone over-train.)

This has been A Word of Caution from the:
ATTBYDFAAA
(Always Think Twice Before You Do or Feel Anything At All Association)

Dear Elizabeth,

I just wanted to say sorry for leaving an anonymous note last week. Maybe it confused you or scared you or something?
   I hope not.

I'm still really really sorry about your dog dying.

A Stranger (Who Catches Your Bus)

ELIZABETH !!!!!

IF YOU THINK OF A SLOGAN FOR RASPBERRY-
FLAVOURED CAT FOOD WHILE YOU'RE EATING
BREAKFAST THIS MORNING, RING ME AT WORK AND
TELL ME.
  TRY REALLY REALLY HARD TO THINK OF ONE!
  AND HAVE A NICE DAY AT SCHOOL.

LOVE,
YOUR
MUM

Dear Mum,

Sorry I didn't ring you at work with a slogan for
raspberry-flavoured cat food. I didn't think of one.
  Hey, I just thought of one. You ready?
RASP-BERRY DELICIOUS!
  What do you reckon? Only I guess you need some
kind of cat angle, huh? You could just add: PURR-
FECTLY NUTRITIOUS!
  Ah well, I guess it's lucky that YOU'RE the one
working in an advertising agency and I'M not.
  I'm going for a run but I'll be back around 7 for
dinner. See you then.

Liz

Dear Elizabeth,

Did you realize that when Arthur Phillip resigned as governor of New South Wales in November 1792, he visited all the farms in the colony and gave each farmer a sheep? Then he sailed home taking along some convicts who were finished being convicts, two Aborigines, four kangaroos and some dingoes?

I'm really sorry that I'm studying for my History exam at the same time as writing to you, but don't you find that weird? I mean, that he took Aborigines and kangaroos back to England with him? I mean, what happened to them?

My Uncle Rosco went to Shanghai once, and he saw a kangaroo in a zoo there. Only it was all by itself in a concrete box as wide as a telephone box and so low that the ceiling almost touched its head. So it couldn't even take one hop or it would knock itself out. There was a dirty window you could look through and see it.

You know what, I think I've changed my mind. I don't want to be one of those Management Consultant people. It must get pretty boring always just telling people to get a move on. I think I'll be a historian so I can find out what happened to people like those Aborigines.

Thanks for your letter. One good thing is that we have finally agreed on food. I agree that your cherry and apricot slice is the best I've ever eaten. Actually, I'm pretty sure I've never eaten cherry and apricot slice before, so that was an easy one, but STILL, it was extremely delicious. Please send me more of your baking.

I have a very important question for you. DO YOU ACTUALLY HAVE A CLASS CALLED LITUR-GICAL DANCE?

That is very, very scary if you do. Maybe I should be rescuing you from that weird school before their satanic rituals brainwash you? Just let me know if you want rescuing, OK?

I don't think you're selfish by the way, but I'll answer your questions anyway. Nothing's happening with me except I'm doing a lot of extra babysitting and a lot of extra shifts at my mum's florist shop. I guess breaking up with Derek has made me Responsible and Mature.

The weird thing now is that I can't figure out WHY I broke up with Derek, but at the same time I don't know whether I should try and get him back – or if he'd take me anyway. All I want to do now is think about him. I don't want to see him or talk to him. I just want space to think about him, and the first time he touched my hand (lending me a pen in a Science exam). And the way he used to make his face go '*yeah, right*' when I said maybe he'd prefer to spend a Saturday night on his own without me. And the way he used to make me punch his stomach so he could show how built up it was, and the way we always had this conversation when he was about to go to the gym:

'What are you doing this arvo?'

'Going to the gym.'

'What are you going to work on?'

'Shoulders.'

What's so great about that conversation? It's an embarrassing conversation, huh? It just used to be kind of offhand, kind of casual. It always made me feel like his shoulders *belonged* to me. You know?

All I want to do now is just be left alone so I can think about his body and the second time we had sex.

The second time was so much better because the idea hadn't really occurred to me that we could do it again. You know, everything seemed to be about the FIRST TIME. So two days after the first time, I was over at his place, and we were kind of shy of each other, pretending nothing had happened. We were in Derek's bedroom sitting on the floor by his bed, drinking hot chocolate and talking about school and stuff, and then his mother put her head around the door and said, 'Just going to K-mart; back in about an hour'. And suddenly I just thought: my God, I really want to try that SEX thing again.

I guess Derek was thinking the same thing because he didn't waste any time. And it was excellent, like I really FELT everything that was happening, and we were just smiling at each other and kissing and everything. Until the condom broke, of course. That bit wasn't so great.

But I can't ever, ever be alone. I have to share my room with Renee, and she tries really hard to be quiet, and keep all her stuffed turtles away from my side. But sometimes I go into my room and I just want to KILL her for existing. She spilt sparkly nail polish all over my dressing table the other day and I shouted at her, which just makes me hate myself. Especially because she's been getting this nervous stomach thing a lot lately – like she's always feeling sick because it's so important to her that she pleases people. She even tried to give me her favourite heart-shaped hairclip so that I would forgive her.

Anyway, so that's the thing – all I want to do now is

think about Derek, and I can't do it unless I'm alone. I mean how can you think about the first time your boyfriend touched you with your little sister in the same room reading out fairytales to her silkworms? How can you think about the second time you had sex, while your dad's standing right beside you drying the dishes?

MEANWHILE, my cousin Maddie's acting like the galaxy just organized a surprise party for her. Seriously, she's DELIRIOUS with happiness. It's like she's feverish or something. It's because she got that guy she wanted – the one who liked her singing voice, but then it turned out he wasn't interested in a relationship, so it was like this huge challenge for Maddie. She's used to guys just sprinting to her door when she blinks at them. She finally won him at a dance party (some guy's 16th birthday party on a yacht of course – that's how you spend your teen years if you live in Double Bay) – she's a fantastic dancer. Anyway, so now he's her boyfriend and he's like diamond standard value because he was so hard to get.

I guess he must be worth a lot, anyway. He's paying for Maddie to take parachuting lessons, to help her get over the trauma of watching her previous boyfriend hang-glide into the side of a cliff. She *was* pretty traumatized – Uncle Rosco and Auntie Belinda had been waking up in the middle of the night to the sounds of Maddie jumping up and down on her bed and shouting, 'Stay away from the edge of the mattress! The floor is a long way down!'

I'd better go because my History exam's on in five minutes. Did you know that one of the first convicts to come to Australia was a SEVENTY-YEAR-OLD woman

155

who stole 12 pounds of CHEESE? I wonder if it was Kraft Slices or Coon Mature Cheddar?

Have fun.

Love,
Christina

ELIZABETH !!!

GUESS WHAT SLOGAN WE USED FOR THE CAT FOOD???

PURR-FECTLY NUTRITIOUS, RASP-BERRY DELICIOUS.

YOU SEE? YOU'RE A GENIUS AFTER ALL. ALL YOU NEEDED WAS MY TRAINED EYE TO SEE THE GENIUS IN YOUR WORK AND SWAP YOUR PHRASES AROUND.

I WANT TO TAKE YOU OUT TO DINNER THIS WEEKEND TO SAY THANK YOU. OK?

YOU ARE WONDERFUL.

LOVE,
YOUR MUM

Dear my mum,

Thanks for your note. How much do I get for writing your copy for you? I would love to go out to dinner with you this weekend. Don't forget I'm going out with Dad on Saturday though.

I'm going to do a hill workout on Foxall Road. I'll be back around 8. See you,

Elizabeth

Dear Elizabeth,

I just realized that the note I left the other day was also an anonymous note.

I'm sorry about leaving an anonymous note apologizing for leaving an anonymous note.

A Stranger Who Catches Your Bus

Dear Christina,

No, I didn't know that Arthur Phillip gave everybody a sheep when he resigned. That was pretty nice of him, wasn't it? Although maybe they'd have preferred a box of chocolates. I'd have preferred a box of chocolates to a sheep. I can't believe he took Aborigines and kangaroos home with him too, as if they were souvenirs.

Hey, I keep forgetting to tell you. A very weird thing is happening to me. I've been getting ANONYMOUS NOTES in my school bag. They're signed 'a stranger who catches your bus' and I keep finding them when I get home from school. Weird, huh? The first one just said, 'Sorry about your dog dying', so I suppose the person must have overheard me telling Celia and Saxon about my dog. Then after that was an apology for sending an anonymous note, and then an apology for sending an anonymous apology. It could go on for ever.

So catching the bus is really strange now. It's strange in a background kind of way because I know that somewhere on the bus there's an Anonymous Person who's feeling guilty about sending me Anonymous

157

Notes. It makes me feel like my shoulders are sticking out a bit too far from my body. Strange, no? Also every time I sneeze or laugh I think, 'What did that sneeze (or laugh) sound like to the Anonymous Person? Did they think it was crass/cute/ridiculous/disgusting? Or did they not notice?'

And it's also strange, catching the bus, because of Celia and Saxon. They always sit together and I always feel like I'm saying the wrong thing, and like they're taking little glances at each other when I do. Then I get mad and lose my temper about something stupid and then I have to pretend I was only joking about being mad. For example, this arvo they were talking about this movie (which they'd seen together) and I said I didn't like it, and they do this quick little glance at each other, this quick little woo-hoo! eyebrow raise at each other. Then Celia's: 'Really? You didn't like it? How come exactly?' and Saxon's: 'Yeah? What's not to like?' Then I started getting furious saying it was inane, superficial crap (even though I didn't think it was THAT bad). It doesn't help – getting mad. It only makes their connection even closer, like sane Saxon and Celia versus crazy Elizabeth.

It's like I've been catching this bus all year and things keep changing – Celia catches it with me and is my best friend; next thing Celia's gone and I'm by myself; next thing Saxon's sitting beside me talking about training and Celia (he talked about Celia so much – what kind of idiot was I not to realize he liked her all the time?); next thing Celia's back and she and Saxon are sitting together every day. Every day I'm there in the same seat and all around me other people's lives are taking all these twists and loops like a ribbon dancer at the Olympics.

So, this letter has been my Essay on Catching the Bus. Maybe I should ask Mr Botherit if he wants a copy as a substitute for my essay on the *Lord of the Flies*. (I'm going to write a letter about that one anyway. I've seen the movie and it's way too violent for me to be reading the book or writing an essay on.)

I'm training a lot for the Forest Hill Half Marathon at the moment, but probably won't do very well. I did a hill workout yesterday, which is where you run up and down a hill over and over to try and strengthen your lower leg muscles. Also to build up endurance. Now my lower leg muscles feel like water tanks. I don't know what my endurance feels like because I don't think I have any.

I had this dream last night that I would get the time which lets you qualify for the Boston Marathon. You have to run a certain time in another marathon before you can even compete in that race; it's like the biggest race in the world. So, since all dreams come true I guess that's what's going to happen. HA HA. (My actual plan is to win the New York Marathon – that one's also hugely famous – and then have the Boston people begging me to join in their marathon because they need me for the publicity.)

Thanks for answering my questions. I really like it when you talk about yourself, and tell me the things you're thinking about. It makes me feel closer to you. I wish I knew what you should do about Derek. It sounds like you really need time to work it out, but it must be impossible with all those kids around. Maybe you and I should swap places? I've got way too much space for thinking at my home. I'm practically always alone. Maybe you should come over and stay at my place –

we've even got a spare room (sorry, I don't mean to show off) and you could just sit in there and THINK. If you can't do that, is there anywhere else you can be alone? Like climbing a tree or something? Or you could take up running. That's when I do all my thinking. Actually, I don't know how I'd ever work out any problems, or avoid going completely crazy, if I didn't have running.

And what's Derek acting like now? Is he being cold or friendly to you? What's it like seeing him when you're at school?

I don't actually see Celia and Saxon at school very much – my only conversations with them are on the bus really. At school, they seem to disappear into the furniture; they're sitting so close together and they both wear all black now, and they just lean their heads together, hide behind Celia's hair, and whisper to each other. So they're easy to miss unless you trip over them. They've stopped talking to anyone else and actually look outraged if anyone dares to try and get their attention.

So how was your History exam? Did you get asked how many kangaroos Governor Phillip took back to England with him? And how was your weekend? Still working in your mum's shop like a good, thoughtful, mature, exemplary teenager?

My weekend was a bit draining. Both of my parents wanted to take me to dinner on Saturday night which turned into a kind of third world war – with Dad saying things like, 'All I ask, all I ask' and Mum saying things like, 'You think you can just step right back into her life?' and me saying things like: 'Uh, couldn't I just stay at home?'

My dad won in the end because he got in first, so he was especially zippy at the restaurant. He asked me if I'd ever been in a mosh pit and said that from above, those things look like screen savers on a computer – a constant movement of crowd surfers sliding towards the front and getting thrown out the side door. Excuse me, but how does my father know what a mosh pit looks like from above?

We had white wine and I said it smelt like nail polish remover. That turned out to be the wrong answer. In FACT, it smelled like green apple peel and butterscotch. What was I thinking?

I had a mother-and-daughter day on Sunday as compensation prize for my mum, and we played tennis and then saw a movie, so that was fine. It's easier with my mum. Neither of us feels like we have to talk unless something comes into our heads. We even talked about Celia a bit, and how much she's changed. And then we spent about an hour planning an imaginary trip to New York because Mum's dying to go there and I want to check out the New York Marathon. I plan to win it before my 21st birthday, so I've got to start getting to know the route. Mum even said she'd walk it with me, except only if we can take a thermos and a picnic basket, and stop at a café or an art gallery every fifteen minutes or so.

Gotta go. Mum just walked in the door and she wants us to go choose a video together. Maybe she's taking this new mother–daughter thing a bit far?

You have fun too,

Love,
Elizabeth

161

Dearest Elizabeth,

Saturday nights at restaurants with your father? Sundays playing
tennis and seeing movies with your mother? Elizabeth! Your
weekends are filled with parents! Your memories will be nothing
but Family Events! Perhaps we can help – it is important that
you do not forget.

Take, for example, Sunday afternoons. Consider, Elizabeth,
the smell of jasmine and barbecues. A magpie on a wire and a
spring blue sky. You hear an ice cream truck play a distorted
tune. You are ten years old, Elizabeth, and what do you
remember?

You remember a Sunday afternoon with Celia on the steps,
and how Celia pretended the steps were an ice castle, and next
she decided she wanted a snail, and sent you out on a snail-
hunting mission. And next you heard the ice cream truck and
ran. You remember how back then, you and she were exactly
the same height, and she had short blonde hair and you had
short dark hair, and the ice cream man said, 'What'll it be,
BOYS?' And you were both so mad that you said, 'NOTHING!'

And then you were back on the steps and even madder
because you had no ice cream.

Kindest regards,
Memory Trigger Society

ELIZABETH !!!

GOOD MORNING TO YOU!
    CAN WE TAKE A RAINCHECK ON THAT TEN-PIN
BOWLING IDEA TONIGHT?
    I FORGOT I HAVE EXTRA ALEXANDER TECHNIQUE

162

CLASSES THIS WEEK, BECAUSE YOUR FATHER HAS
MADE MY NECK START CRUNCHING AGAIN.
  THERE'S A COLD CHANGE COMING TODAY SO <u>TAKE
YOUR JUMPER.</u>

LOVE,
YOUR MUM

Dear Elizabeth,

I don't know what to do. I'm experiencing extreme
complications of guilt. I keep sending you anonymous
notes apologizing about anonymous notes and then
straight away I have to apologize for anonymous
apologizing. It's like a corkscrew that keeps winding
itself in and out of its loops. It's like when you're
playing tennis and you keep hitting the ball into the
net and saying, 'Sorry', and your opponent gets
annoyed and says, 'Quit saying sorry', and then the
next time you hit the ball into the net you say, 'Sorry',
and then you remember you're not supposed to say
sorry so you say, 'Oh, sorry'.
  You get what I mean?
  So maybe I could make this the Final Apology? I
mean, within this letter could I apologize for sending
this apology? You see what I mean? When you get off
the bus maybe you could give some kind of a signal that
this is OK? Maybe you could hop twice or something
once you get off the bus and I'll watch from the
window?
  I don't want to stop being anonymous and tell you

163

who I am, because I'm too embarrassed. But as a compromise I could REDUCE my anonymity by telling you a BIT about who I am.

OK? I'm very sorry.

From:

A Stranger Who Catches Your Bus, and Who Sits up
the Back, and Who Goes to Brookfield.
(Is that enough? Sorry.)

Dear Elizabeth,

I'm writing from home today which is strange. I feel like I've brought you into my room to show you around. The bed with the black duvet on it is mine, by the way. The one with the twirling ballerinas and pink ruffles is Renee's. You guessed that anyway, right?

It was raining all morning and now the girls who live next door are out weeding their pear trees. Do you weed pear trees? Maybe they're pruning them. They've got an orchard right in their front yard, and they've come out wearing enormous straw hats and sun dresses and crouched down beside the trees to work, and it's like we're in another century. It's fantastic.

We used to have a vegetable farm too, but then Dad sold it so he could try and set up his front-loader business, and Mum got her florist shop in Baulkham Hills. And Dad's front-loader business turned out to be a monumental flop, but Mum's florist shop flourished. HA.

I can also see the dog from the neighbours on the other side trying to get the attention of the next-door-neighbour girls in their hats. That dog has some serious issues. As soon as he sees anybody in the neighbourhood come out of their house, he comes hurtling towards them and throws himself at their feet. Literally. He just tosses himself onto the ground, puts his chin right onto the grass, and *wails* at you to pay attention. Then if you're nice to him, he cries and turns onto his back and makes you scratch him. It's strange, but it makes everyone hate him – it's kind of like, 'Have some pride, dog! Get up onto your feet and put your head in the air!'

I'm sorry. I hope talking about dogs doesn't upset you. I'm sure your dog Lochie was proud and beautiful. You can send me a photo if you want to? I'd send it straight back.

You know how you said that it feels like you're staying still on the bus while everything changes around you? That's wild, because it's quite common to be sitting on a bus and feeling like the bus is standing still while the trees and letter boxes slide on past the windows. But you're normally WRONG if you think that, because in fact you're sliding along the road and the post boxes are just standing there.

Only this time you're RIGHT – you ARE standing still and everything else IS moving. INTERESTING.

But why is it interesting?

I don't know.

Sorry.

I just wasted a lot of your time.

Oh, HEY. Read this bit because it's important and I think you have a Right to Know. You know your anonymous notes? Guess what. I know who's writing them. You remember I told you a really good friend of mine catches your bus and he's the one who described to me what you look like? Remember he said you looked like an elf with your funny ears, and Celia looked like a fairy princess about to fly out the window? Well, he's always asking how you are because he knows I write to you, so one time when he asked I told him about your dog. Don't worry, I didn't tell him about anything else – just that your dog died. My God, he was SO UPSET. He seriously had tears in his eyes. He was really worried about you. (He asks about you a LOT actually – I think he might have a crush on you.)

So when you told me someone was leaving you anonymous notes I thought of him and made him confess. So that's who it is. Sorry if he's annoying you.

Gotta go because the baby's crying, and I think by the way Renee's yelling that Robbo might be ripping into the couch with the kitchen scissors.

Love,
Christina

Dear Elizabeth,

Ha. Mystery solved.

The anonymous note-writer is no longer anonymous. He's just some friend of Christina's.

Provisional offer unprovisionally withdrawn.

Don't expect to hear from US again.

The Secret and Mysterious Association of All That is Secret and Mysterious

Dear Elizabeth,

Still.

    Some mysterious boy has a crush on you.

    We await further developments with interest.

Sincerely,
Young Romance Association

Dear Elizabeth,

So, here's what we have.

    He talked about Celia floating away like a kite.

    So he is poetic.

    He says sorry too much when he plays tennis.

    So he plays tennis.

    He likes dogs.

    He seems smart.

    He wanted you to signal him when you got off the bus, so he must get off at a stop after you.

    He has a guilt complex.

    So which one is he? Figure it out.

Yours, in anticipation,
Society of Amateur Detectives

Dear Elizabeth,

You are on the bus. Neither Saxon nor Celia are here to distract you with their giggling and murmuring. Celia must have been

167

too ill to come to school and Saxon has probably rushed to her side like the noble suitor that he is.

That is by the by.

The important thing is this: use the opportunity.

Who sits at the back of the bus?

Five Brookfield boys.

Consider your options.

One is loud, wears a lot of Adidas, is always tapping the top of his cigarette pack, and has dirty old trainers way out in the aisle for people to trip over.

One has black hair, black eyes and a grunge leather jacket, and enormous boots which are also jamming up the aisle.

Look away! Act like a detective!

OK, look back again.

One has blond curly hair and cheekbones, good God, the cheekbones, and a loud laugh that makes old women turn around.

One is feral. Half his head is shaved and the other half is dreads. His nose is pierced twice. How did he do that?

And one leans forward on his elbows and speaks the soft lines that make the blond one laugh.

So which one is he? Figure it out.

Yours, a little impatiently,
Society of Amateur Detectives

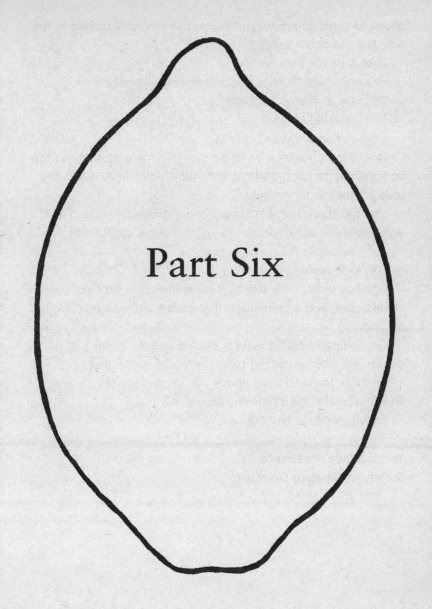

Part Six

ELIZABETH !

CELIA'S MUM CALLED ME AT WORK TODAY. IT TURNS
OUT CELIA DISAPPEARED IN THE NIGHT AGAIN LAST
NIGHT. HAVE YOU HEARD FROM HER?

HER MOTHER WAS A BIT HYSTERICAL. I GUESS
CELIA MUST BE FINALLY SENDING HER OVER THE
EDGE. I HAVE NOTICED THAT HER BREATHING SOUNDS
MORE ASTHMATIC THAN SERENE LATELY. MAYBE YOU
SHOULD GIVE HER A CALL?

LOVE,
YOUR MUM

Dear Elizabeth,

I'm assuming that was just a joke. You realize that Celia has
disappeared again? You realize this could be SERIOUS? And
your immediate reaction is, 'Who gives a damn? I've got to run
15k today and there's only one month till the Forest Hill Half
Marathon'.

Excuse me, Elizabeth, but even if your 'Who gives a damn?'
WAS a joke, this is simply not a laughing matter.

Please proceed immediately to Celia's house and ascertain the
circumstances of her disappearance.

Sincerely,
Best Friends Club

Dear Christina,

Your last letter was just like being invited into your home. I could actually SEE through your window – the pear trees and the hats and the obsequious dog. (In the previous sentence you will notice an example of my new vocabulary – our English teacher is giving us a Word A Day.) You're a fantastic letter-writer, you know. Thanks for having me over.

And you're right too, my dog NEVER grovelled like that. Lochie was proud and magnificent. I'm enclosing a photo which demonstrates that. I wonder how come your neighbour's dog is so desperate? What are its owners like? I hope they don't beat it up or something? Maybe it's just that that dog's a peasant-dog and my dog was nobility.

Guess what? Celia's run away again. I know, surprise, surprise. She disappeared in the night last night, taking the family cuckoo clock with her. But when we phoned Saxon's family it turned out that *he's* vanished too. So nobody's especially worried, except Saxon's parents and they're having a joint apoplectic fit. Celia's mum was a bit frantic at first, because Celia's still sick so she's too fragile to be joining more circuses. Plus because Celia's brother Ben tried to join the navy last week (they rejected his application – he's thirteen years old) – so the family stress levels were up.

But as soon as she found out that Saxon was gone too, she told everyone to chill out because Saxon would take care of her. My mum said if I ever thought about running away with a sixteen-year-old guy I better not expect her to chill out.

I wonder when I'll hear from Celia this time. Maybe

never. Maybe she'll never come back. Maybe Saxon's all she needs.

So now the bus has changed again and I'm catching it alone. Hey, thanks for telling me who the Anonymous Notewriter is. You are a True Friend. It was driving me crazy. Though of course, now it's driving me crazier.

Can you tell your friend thanks for the note about my dog and he can stop apologizing for his apologies if he wants? But how come he has to stay anonymous? Tell him he should keep feeling guilty about that and sending me apologies won't help. Because it's not fair. He knows what I look like and I don't know what he looks like.

Maybe *you* could just give me a clue. There are five Brookfield guys down the back of the bus. One has bad skin, wears a lot of Adidas, and carries a pack of cigarettes and a mean frown; one's kind of grunge with dark hair which he pushes out of his eyes all the time with a look on his face like he's surprised it keeps falling back down; one's blond and loud and has beautiful cheekbones and a really crazy laugh; one's feral and has scabby elbows; and one's quiet, but he must be funny because he makes the others laugh.

Can't you just give me one clue? Yesterday something strange was going on down the back. It was something to do with the quiet guy having said something wrong – I think he must have insulted the one with the Adidas and the cigarette pack. Maybe he made a joke about his clothes? Cigarette boy was talking to him in this low-down ominous voice, like a snake sliding underneath the bus seats. The whole bus was bristling with tension, and everyone was sitting perfectly still trying to hear what he was saying.

Blond boy was doing his loud crazy laugh in an attempt to switch off the tension, but it just intensified the feeling that something brutal was about to happen, because it's so manic, his laugh.

Grunge boy was staring out the window.

Quiet boy was just nodding along to everything Cigarette boy was saying, just agreeing, like, 'Absolutely, absolutely, absolutely'. Which didn't seem to be helping, because Cigarette boy's low words were building up and up like a truck getting onto a highway.

Finally, Feral boy took control of the situation, turned his back on Quiet boy, put his arm around Cigarette boy's neck, and started talking to him at high speed.

It seemed to work, because then Quiet boy said something else quiet and Cigarette boy kind of half-smiled, Feral boy hit them both on the back of their heads, and everything was OK. The bus driver changed gears and the bus relaxed.

But you see my dilemma? I didn't know which one I was supposed to be backing. What if next time they start fighting it turns into this huge rumble and they all come tumbling down the aisle beating each other up? What if one of them lands right by my seat? How will I know whether to knock him out with my school bag or put a cold steak against his black eye?

More importantly, where will I find a cold steak?

My dad wants to take me on a YACHT this Saturday. He was really pleased with the idea because it will be introducing VARIETY into our father–daughter relationship. I have a feeling a yacht's probably exactly the same as an exclusive restaurant except that it floats.

And my mum wants to take me to aqua-aerobics with her on Sunday. It's her competitive thing – if Dad can get me ONTO water, she can go one step further and get me INTO water. I don't know when they expect me to get any homework done. Not that I ever do any anyway, but still. What if I wanted to recreate myself as academically inclined?

Talking about homework, my English teacher's given us a weird assignment. We're studying *My Brilliant Career* at the moment and instead of getting us to write an essay on it he wants us to write a letter explaining why we shouldn't be writing an essay. I can't work out whether this is some wacky new teaching method, or a conspiracy to get me to write an essay. Either way he stole the idea from me.

Maybe I'll just write a letter explaining why I shouldn't write a letter?

That reminds me, maybe YOU should write a letter to Derek explaining how you feel? How DO you feel about him now? Or maybe not. Letters don't always work. I wrote to my Canadian stepbrother WEEKS ago now, and he's just ignored me. So that's embarrassing.

God, I just remembered I had to go to the library today and photocopy a map of Africa and colour in the deserts and jungles and cities in different colours and it's due right after lunch and the end of lunchtime bell's ringing as we speak. Have to go.

Actually, are you kidding? I'm not going to do that Africa thing. I think I'll just explain that I learned colouring-in back in Year 1, thanks all the same.

But I'd better go anyway. Have lots of fun and eat something delicious for breakfast tomorrow.

Lots of love,
Elizabeth

Elizabeth,

Welcome to the afternoon bus. Assume your undercover agent
persona. Use your fist to wipe away the dust on the window,
and watch through the window with a casual, dreamy
expression as the Brookfield kids beat each other up to get
aboard.

OK. Grunge boy is first and he's carrying a tennis racket.
Think, Elizabeth. Tennis racket. Tennis player.
It's him. It's Grunge boy.
Interestingly, Feral boy also has a tennis racket sticking out of
his bag.
Ah. I see Quiet boy and Blond boy have rackets too.
I guess it must have been sports day at Brookfield today, huh?

Yours with some irritation,
Society of Amateur Detectives

Elizabeth,

Cigarette boy just got off the bus. BEFORE YOU.
It's not him.
Try not to feel quite so elated. This is a serious breakthrough
in a serious assignment.

Yours with a stern reprimand,
Society of Amateur Detectives

ELIZABETH !!!

I FORGOT TO TELL YOU LAST NIGHT. YOUR FATHER
E-MAILED ME AT WORK AND SAID YOU SHOULD BRING
A WINDCHEATER ON THE YACHT TOMORROW. WHEN
YOU SEE HIM YOU SHOULD REMIND HIM THAT
THERE'S A PHONE RIGHT HERE IN OUR HOUSE WHERE
HE CAN LEAVE MESSAGES FOR YOU. WHY DOES HE
KEEP CONTACTING ME AT WORK? YOU SHOULD ALSO
REMIND HIM THAT 'WINDCHEATER' IS A WORD FROM
AN ENTIRELY OTHER ERA.

DON'T RUN TOO FAR TODAY; I WANT TO MAKE YOU
A SPECIAL LEMON SOUFFLÉ FOR DESSERT TONIGHT
AND WE CAN WATCH A VIDEO. THE RECIPE FOR THE
LEMON SOUFFLÉ IS IN THE BOTTOM DRAWER AND
YOU'RE WELCOME TO BEGIN IT AT ANY POINT.

DON'T OVERDO THE RUNNING. IT'S SUPPOSED TO BE
EXTREMELY HOT TODAY, AND AREN'T YOU TRAINING
A BIT TOO MUCH THESE DAYS?

HEARD FROM CELIA YET?

LOVE,
YOUR MUM

Mum,

I'm running down Glenhaven Road to Dural if you feel
like driving over with a fresh water bottle for me. Yes,
it's too hot to be running and dehydration is a serious
issue.

I made the lemon soufflé and it's in the fridge ready

for baking. Don't start it because I want to monitor the baking process. If you start it and it collapses it's your own responsibility and I will have to kill you.

See you soon,
Liz

P.S. No, I haven't heard from Celia yet. How about you?

Dearest Elizabeth,

Recently, Housewives of the World United sent your file to us, and we were decidedly impressed. We have been toying with the possibility of offering you membership in our association, much as one toys with a sticky caramel in one's mouth.

It is your conduct this evening, however, that has clinched the decision for us, much as a dusting of walnut pieces might clinch the success of a rich chocolate cake.

Elizabeth, we were gobsmacked.

Never before have we witnessed a first-time soufflé so golden, so gilded, so aureate! Never have we seen a first-time soufflé so light, so airy, so feathery! Never have we endured the delirious, mouthwatering anguish of a first-time soufflé rising with the grandeur of a mountain of strawberry ice!!!

We implore you to accept our offer of membership, much as a grandmother might implore a skinny grandchild to accept her offer of a thick slice of meatloaf.

Please do say yes or we will weep salty tears into our pastry.

Yours ever,
Chefs 'R Supreme, much like the pizza

Dear Elizabeth,

Monday mornings are like hell really, aren't they? God, when my clock radio starts shouting at me on a Monday morning I really want to kill it. You know, crush it with my fist like a hammer.

I hate mornings.

It's unfair how quickly you get out of the habit of getting up too. I mean, all you do is sleep in for two weekend days, and next thing it's Monday and your body's going, 'Uh, this is like four hours before getting up time or something; you want to turn off that noise and go back to sleep?'

Anyway, right now the only thing stopping me from falling into a coma on my desk is writing to you. Thanks. It's a combination of the Monday-morning-tiredness thing and the most-boring-man-in-the-world-congratulations-come-on-down Rattlesnake. Rattlesnake is Mr Rivers, our stupendous Science teacher, and I don't think it's fair that he gets to be called a cool name like Rattlesnake. It started because people thought he was so thick there was all this space in his brain with bits of gravel rattling around in there. So they called him Rattles. And then it turned into Rattlesnake, a cool-ification which I really resent.

Derek's in this class too. He's sitting right up the front because he was being a Distraction up the back. I think it was a mistake moving him up the front because he can be even more of a Distraction there. His smart comments are perfectly audible. In fact, Rattlesnake keeps losing his concentration, stamping one foot, and rubbing out scientific symbols from the blackboard. Everyone's getting annoyed because they have to cross

179

out what they just wrote down. Serves them right for copying it straight down like that.

I still can't work out what I feel about Derek. Even right here in this class, one minute I'm, 'Oh my God, that was so funny what he just said, I love him so much,' and next minute I'm, 'What a stupid, smart-arsed thing to say; he's such a walrus.' We hardly speak to each other any more except if we practically bump into each other, and then we're just polite. But every now and then I catch him looking over at me with this tiny little hurt crumple in his forehead.

Every now and then I also see Katrina Ecclehurst twirling her ponytail in his face and leaning up close to him to say, 'Whatcha doing this weekend, Derry?'

or

'Whatcha doing for the History assignment, Dezza?'

or

'You going to the Carlingford dance, Dekko?'

She's going to seriously wind up with some H_2SO_4 up her nose if she keeps that up.

It's completely unlike me to be so indecisive about a guy – usually I make up my mind in about one tenth of a second and take action.

Anyway, this is boring for you. I prefer to think about you really. Guess who else is in my Science class right now and sitting here beside me? You guessed it – Mr Anonymous-Note-Writer-Extraordinaire. He's a serious wreck. I just told him I was writing to you and he went into severe panic mode. He practically climbed out the window just then to avoid you seeing him. He really has a crush on you – oh wait . . .

Sorry. I thought he was trying to see what I was saying so I had to stop. He just wanted to borrow my Tippex.

He's doing some artwork on the back of my Science folder and he wanted white for the clouds. Anyway, he's terrified that you'll find out who he is because he's so embarrassed about ever starting anything. He says you're an engaging phantasm and he can't stop writing poetry about you. He thinks you should be a film star. He says your pixie face and elfin ears would send any movie producer into ecstasies.

I told him that you think it's unfair for him to be anonymous and he agreed absolutely. But he says he can't see a way around it.

Still, I've decided that I'm on your side more than his. So I'm going to give you three clues.

Clue No. 1. His first name begins with a 'J'.

Clue No. 2. He's also in my Home Ec class and we made chocolate muffins today.

Clue No. 3. You know how there's a blond guy with a wacky laugh who's on your bus? Well, that's who it is.

HA.

That was just a joke. It's definitely not him. He's off the planet, that blond guy. I don't know what he's on but it's something serious, and so is his anorexic girlfriend. She's got dark circles around her eyes and her elbows are so skinny the bones are going to break through any moment.

I better go because this class is almost over and I should start writing some of this crap into my folder. It'll just fall right out though. Papers never stay in my folder.

How was the yacht trip with your dad (and you tried to tell me you weren't a nice private school girl) and the aqua-aerobics with your mum? I wonder if you should just tell your mum that she doesn't need to compete because you'll always like her best. Because that's true, isn't it – you do like her the best? Then maybe she can relax.

Still, it's nice that she's spending time with you, isn't it. She might have been leaving you alone a bit too much before.

I HAVE to go.

God, I forgot about Celia. The disappearing thing must get boring for you I guess – but I can't believe she ran away with Saxon. Are you OK about that – do you think you're over Saxon now? I also can't believe that her mother's OK with it. It hurts my mind trying to imagine how my parents would react if I did that.

GOTTA go.

You eat something delicious too,

Love,
Christina

Dear Elizabeth,

My conscience is sending me off the edge. I shouldn't have started this. Christina says you think it's wrong that I'm anonymous and you are so completely right. The more I make excuses the further off the edge I'll go.

Tomorrow morning I am going to get on the bus wearing a black cap.

Best wishes,
A Stranger

Elizabeth!

Tomorrow, you will know!

Work quickly, Elizabeth and see if you can beat the clock! If you guess before the Black Cap tomorrow you will have a fortunate and happy life and will probably win the half marathon. We offer you that in return for rapid detective work.

So which one is it, Elizabeth? Figure it out.

It is not Cigarette boy. (Hooray!)

It is not Blond boy. (Hooray!)

OK, hush now with your cheering and frivolity.

Therefore, it could be Feral boy, Grunge boy, or Quiet boy.

Which one, Elizabeth?

His name begins with a 'J'. So listen.

He made chocolate muffins today. So watch.

Good God, Feral boy is boarding the bus with a muffin in his hand.

It's him then.

It's Feral boy.

OK. Fine.

Although, of course, Anonymous boy could have GIVEN Feral boy a muffin.

Ha. For example, Cigarette boy is now boarding the bus with half a chocolate muffin in his mouth. (The bus driver is speaking to him which is a mistake – yes, a mistake – he is answering and chocolate muffin is cascading to the floor.)

So. Listen.

You heard what Cigarette boy just said as he moved down the aisle with the rest of the muffin showering around him. You heard it.

'Get a move on, Johnno.'

That's what he said.

To whom was he speaking?

183

To Feral boy who was walking before him in the aisle, or to Quiet boy behind him taking time with his bus pass?

To whom did he speak?

Which one is Johnno?

And even if you knew which one was Johnno, does that mean that none of the others have names beginning with a 'J'?

You are beginning to frustrate us.

Give it some more thought and then get back to us, hmm?

Yours, a little irritably,
Society of Amateur Detectives

Dear Christina,

Look. Just because my dad can borrow a yacht from a rich friend doesn't mean I'm a nice private school girl. Can we get that cleared up for good? Besides, this yacht looked more like a row boat with a sail to me. It was tiny. Completely overcrowded once it had my dad, me and a picnic basket on board.

Still, it was kind of fun. I was impressed that my dad could sail a boat, and sailing kept him busy so he didn't try so hard to impress me. Interesting. It's a bit scary, sailing – I had to help sometimes and had no idea what was going on. Like winding ropes around things and then unwinding them and ducking your head out of the way and climbing from one side to the other. All at superfast speed. It was such a beautiful day though, and we went right in to the harbour, and the sun practically melted into the ripples of water, while the breeze washed against our faces. The picnic basket included ham sandwiches, a packet of Mint Slices, and a bottle of lemonade, which was a shock. I was expecting smoked salmon and chardonnay.

I wanted to ask Dad about my Canadian stepbrother, without actually admitting that I'd written a letter to him. So I said, 'Is your Canadian family ever coming over to visit you?'

Dad said, 'Nope. Too far. See if you can untie that knot there, would you?'

So much for that. I'll just have to give up on my long-lost, never-met stepbrother, I suppose.

After we got back to Dad's car I suddenly remembered that we were at Double Bay. And Double Bay is where Dad's living now.

So I asked if we could see his place.

He gave me that panicked look of his again, and concentrated on doing up his seat belt.

Then I said, 'Couldn't we at least DRIVE past it?'

He concentrated on the gear stick and the dashboard for a while, frowned at his keys for a while longer, and finally turned the key in the ignition.

Then I said again, 'Dad? Couldn't we just drive past your place?'

I hardly ever call him 'Dad'. Usually, I don't call him anything. It seems to have a powerful effect when I do, so I keep it in reserve.

He started driving without talking and I wondered if I had to say it again. But out of nowhere he's saying in a mumble, 'This is my street.'

And next thing we've started accelerating up a hill and he's waving one arm fast and saying, 'That's my place.'

We were past it in a quarter of a second. What's WITH him anyway? All that I got to see was a flash of

185

white behind fantastic red bougainvillea, and what I think was a verandah with a windsurfer and a surfboard on it.

I'm not sure. But I think so.

This is my mum when I got home: 'Your father is ALWAYS getting you sunburnt like this. Your father is an IRRESPONSIBLE parent. Your father will have you in hospital with skin cancer before you've finished high school.'

Anyway, I told her about driving past Dad's place and the windsurfer and surfboard, and she said, 'Well doesn't that just figure. Boys and their toys. Second childhood, only he never grew out of his first one.'

Things like that.

The next day Mum took me to her aqua-aerobics class and we did very strange things in a small swimming pool while a woman shouted at us. I think the woman was making up the instructions as she went along. This kind of thing:

'OK now, jump up and down! Now jump from side to side! Now hold the side of the pool, kick one leg out to the side, blow raspberries and wave your hand in the air!'

It's true that I usually have a better time with my mum, but on this weekend I've got to say that Dad really won hands down.

Although, both my parents are weird. After aerobics when we were all showered and shampooed and I thought we'd just have a relaxing night watching telly, Mum suddenly says, 'Let's go for a drive.'

The entire way to Double Bay she was doing this, 'I'll just take this road here and see where it leads us', and, 'Oh well, look, we may as well drive over the Harbour

Bridge now we're here', and 'Ever seen Vaucluse, Liz? Let's take a look.'

Honestly, some people can be so transparent.

Surprise, surprise, there we were in Double Bay and Mum was saying, 'Hey, isn't this – isn't this where your dad's living now?!'

She wanted me to try and remember where the house was, which of course I couldn't remember, so we drove around Double Bay for over an hour looking. After a while, Mum had to drop her 'Oh, here's a pretty street, let's have a look down here' act, and just focus on hunting down my father.

I finally recognized the street and we slowed right down outside the white house with the bougainvillea. And there were the windsurfer and the surfboard. And then GUESS WHAT HAPPENED?

Oh wait a second, Mum's calling me.

Hi again. Sorry to abandon you like that. It's the next day. Mum wanted me to help her make dinner and then she just wanted to talk all night. I started writing this yesterday afternoon right after I got your letter, and what I hadn't got a chance to say yet was that your anonymous friend promised to identify himself. He left me a note yesterday saying that he'd wear a black cap on the bus. So this MORNING I'm all excited and nervous when I get on the bus. I look down the back at the Brookfield boys, as casual as I could.

And guess what?

Every single one of them was wearing a black cap.

You tell your friend that's not funny. It's a mean trick.

I was so angry I actually looked straight into the eyes of every one of them on the back seat to try and catch him out. But they all just looked at me with mild interest, like, 'Yeah? can I help?' Infuriating is an under-statement.

There was another Event on the bus this morning too. Cigarette boy jumps on (wearing his stupid black cap backwards) and starts to walk up the back, and suddenly the bus driver says, 'Pass?'

Cigarette boy just ignores him and keeps on sauntering down the aisle.

The driver turns right around in his seat and says, 'Bus pass?'

Cigarette boy keeps walking.

The bus is just sitting on the kerb rumbling, the door's still open, and everyone's looking from the driver to the aisle.

Finally, when Cigarette boy's reached the back and sat down in the middle with his legs strung out down the aisle, bus driver half stands and bellows, 'Boy! Did you show me your bus pass?'

Cigarette boy finally answers.

'Yep.'

Bus driver turns around and holds the steering wheel again and the bus rumbles.

Bus driver turns back.

'No you didn't.'

'Yep. I did.'

'Well get back down here and show me again.'

Cigarette boy sits still.

Bus driver stares straight ahead with one eye on the rear view mirror, watching the back of the bus.

Cigarette boy finally stands up, moves slowly back up

the aisle, flips a pass in the driver's face, and turns to walk back again.

Bus driver says, 'That's not your pass.'

Cigarette boy keeps walking to the back and sits down again.

Bus driver says, 'That pass belongs to the dark-haired lad beside you. I saw him give it to you.'

Everyone's looking back now. The dark-haired lad beside him is Grunge boy.

If Grunge boy really gave his pass to Cigarette boy, the driver has sharp eyes. I never saw it and I was watching the whole time.

Bus driver says to Grunge boy, 'Now you show me your pass.'

Feral boy calls out, 'Come on. Give us a break.'

Blond boy calls out, 'We've gotta get to school, sir. We're running late.'

Bus driver sits still for a moment, staring into the rear vision mirror.

Finally, he flaps the door closed, puts the bus in gear and drives down the road.

Anyway, the bus driver got his revenge this afternoon on the way back home from school. This old woman was waiting at a bus stop and the driver stopped and everyone heard the conversation:

'Do you go to Church Street?'

'No, love.'

'I don't mean Church Street, I mean Factory Street.'

'I don't stop till I get to Baulkham Hills, love. Sorry.'

Cigarette boy shouts out from the back of the bus, 'Let her on. Take her where she wants to go.'

Next thing the bus driver's out of his seat and heading down the back.

189

He says, 'Get off the bus.'

Cigarette stares at him.

'You didn't have a pass this morning and you didn't have one this afternoon either. You can walk home.'

The other guys start going, 'Oh, come on, fair go' and stuff like that. But the bus driver just says, 'Off my bus. I'm not moving till you get off my bus.'

So Cigarette says, 'Fine' and gets off. He hits the side of the bus as he walks away, and the driver's face gets so fluorescent it looks like he's going to get out and belt him.

But he doesn't.

We just drive on.

So anyway, at least your friends make the bus trips entertaining. But seriously I was so mad about that black cap thing.

Hey, I never finished telling you the story about driving to Double Bay with my mum. You know how we slowed down outside Dad's house, and saw the surfboard and windsurfer out the front? Well NEXT thing we see a woman walk out of the front door in a swimming costume, shift a deckchair out of the shade, sit back in it, and start to read.

Mum was just, 'Oh my GOD' and driving away fast.

I said, 'It could be just a visitor.'

And Mum said, 'That's no visitor.'

It was true – she looked like she lived there, the way she was so casual with the deckchair and the book.

After a while, Mum said, 'I suppose she came over to see him then.'

And I said, 'Well, no. That can't be his wife. She's still in Canada.'

Then Mum's screeching the car around corners in this frenzy of talking: 'Well. I should have known. If he cheated on me then he'd cheat on HER too. She should have known what she was in for. Once a snake, always a snake. It just figures.' Blah, blah, blah.

So I guess my dad's having an affair.

That explains why he's so determined that I not see his place here I suppose, or meet any of his business associates.

I don't really care since I don't know the person he's cheating on. But my mum seems to REALLY care. She wants to keep talking and talking about it, and her voice is kind of brittle and bright, and she's got this new kind of glittery look in her eye. It's like she's happy, but in a sharp-edged way – like a shiny cheese grater.

This is a long letter, huh? And once again, I've ignored your letter. Wait a minute and I'll look at it again.

Yes, I agree that Monday mornings are awful and I HATE getting up in the mornings. I should really train in the mornings, especially now that it's getting hot in the afternoons, but sleep is way too important to me. So I understand perfectly.

Katrina Ecclehurst sounds like a first-class loser and I really don't think Derek's going to fall for her. At least not until she figures out what his actual name is, anyway. It seems like you could get him back if you wanted to, but maybe it's best to just leave it for a while now? I mean, until you're really sure. It must be awful to be so unsure – I wish I could meet Derek and help you decide.

Of course, I have to meet you first.

Oh yeah, and Celia's still missing and I haven't heard a word. I'm actually trying not to think about her at all – if she wants to disappear from my life, maybe I should just let her?

191

I've got to do my English homework now – I've decided to write the letter about *My Brilliant Career* because I realized that that's my area of expertise and I might actually do well.

See ya,
Elizabeth

Elizabeth,

You must despise me.

I honestly meant to carry through with the black cap idea. Honestly. And then I went into a kind of panic. I went into a frenzy.

I called all the other guys and asked them to wear black caps.

They don't know why, but they think I'm weird anyway, so it's good to occasionally do something inexplicable and sustain the image.

I could have just not worn a cap at all, but that seemed like too much of a cop out.

I have now created a web for myself which I see no way to untangle. I am only sorry to have got you tangled too. I'm going to have to pack up and move interstate.

Tonight, I will call the CIA and ask if they have any spare identities for me to assume.

It is now a matter of national security that you forget my existence.

Forgive me.
A Stranger

Dear Elizabeth,

Which one is it, now?
  Figure it out.

Society of Amateur Detectives

Dearest Lizzy,

Remember how I used to call you Lizard? Remember
how we used to want to tread on lizards' tails to see
them shake free? And then we planned to catch them
to watch their tails grow back, but they always slid away
from us, underneath a rock?

I know we thought we had to do that to the lizards,
because they needed to be trained so they'd know what
to do if a bird attacked. But I guess it wasn't very nice
of us. I guess sometimes people do things that they
think will be good for other people, but then it turns
out they're just being cruel.

Lizzy.

This is the hardest letter I ever had to write.

You are my best friend. You always were and always
will be.

I miss you. Lizzy, remember how we used to play
hopscotch and we drew the longest hopscotch in the
world; we drew it all the way down the street and round
the corner? Remember when your mum brought home
the biggest box of chalk in the world and we thought:
this will last FOR EVER?

I feel as if I have lost you. You are a different person.

193

It's like you've disappeared. Ever since I got back from the circus, it's like you've disappeared.

The Lizzy I used to know would have been so happy for me because I've finally found somebody I love. Saxon is like my dream boy, like my perfect match.

You brought him to me. You found him and you delivered him to me in Coffs Harbour. I was so grateful and happy.

But then something strange happened. You weren't happy for me. You never asked me a single question about Saxon or about how I felt.

Maybe you thought you had to be cruel to me so I'd learn how to survive on my own. But maybe you were being too cruel, Lizzy? Maybe you just weren't being fair?

I don't know why I'm saying all this. Because I don't want you to blame yourself. I want you to know you've always been my best friend in the world.

And I'll always miss you.

But it's not your fault. Please don't believe it's your fault.

It's nobody's fault – not my mum's or my dad's or my brother's, not anyone's.

It's just that Saxon and I have made the decision that we have to make. Because our love is pure like snowflakes. We don't want it to get muddy and grey. We can't see how to live in this world because it's such a vicious world, it's such a dirty, grey, materialistic, unjust and savage world.

So we're going away together. I mean away for good.

I mean tomorrow night we want to just hold hands and jump off the cliff at North Head, OK?

Lizzy, you are my best friend.
Goodbye, OK?

Love always,
Celia

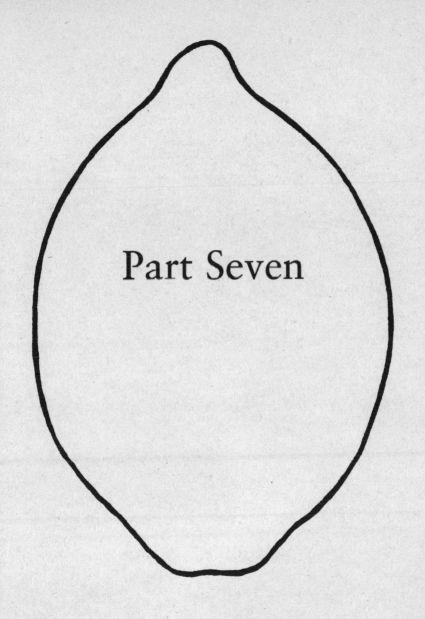

Part Seven

Christina.

I don't know what else to do except write to you.
What else can I do?
I don't know. I can't figure it out.
I think I might throw up.
OK, I have to explain.
I'm in the hospital right now and I'm sitting by Celia, and she tried to kill herself.

God, I can't explain the way I feel. It's different to anything I ever felt before. It's like someone took me by the shoulders and shook me and shook me. So I'm all bedraggled and weak.

Only at the same time, I feel poisoned. Like someone tipped a bottle of poison into my chest.

What happened? I don't know.

I didn't hear anything from Celia for days, and I thought she and Saxon must have moved into a cave and were living happily ever after on roasted seaweed or something. Then suddenly I get this letter from Celia out of nowhere, this letter saying how I'm her best friend, but I'm not there for her any more, and now she and Saxon are going to jump off the cliffs at North Head.

God, I read this letter and I just started shaking.

What does she mean, I'm not there for her? I've been here all along. I'm always here, just waiting for her. I waited for her while she ran away to busk in

Kiama, and when she tried to get a job as a farmhand out at Coonabarabran, and when she – God, so many times. I waited for her when we were eight years old and she ran away to live in the broom closet at the back of our Year 2 classroom.

She was actually angry with me for not being HAPPY for her about Saxon. How far does she want me to go? She expects me to notice that she's found her dream boy, when she didn't even notice all those times that I was looking in my locker for just a little too long, so she wouldn't see that I was crying?

And somehow she's figured out that I'm being deliberately cruel to her so that she will learn to survive on her own? Where does that COME FROM? When have I ever abandoned her? I used to think she was trying to teach *me* to survive on my own. God, I'm so mad I could strangle her right now.

Only she's so tiny and fragile I want to just gather her up into my arms and carry her far away to a safe place with down quilts and fireplaces, and bring her mugs of hot chocolate. I feel like if somebody tried to hurt her, even if somebody tweaked her hair, even if they pinched her arm, I'd put my hands around their throat and just squeeze until they were dead.

I have to calm down.

So I got the letter and I wanted to throw up. I never felt so sick with panic. Actually, the panic started after a moment – at first I just felt dead. I mean I thought she was dead. Then I realized it was that exact night that she wanted to jump and I went into the most intense panic ever.

I phoned Mum at work and they said she was in a meeting and I just hung up. Then I thought, my God, this is an emergency, so I phoned again and made them interrupt the bloody meeting. It was all slow motion, you know? Or like a slow-motion replay, because nothing seemed to happen until after I'd done it.

Then everyone was taking over, and calling the police, and Celia's mum, and Saxon's parents, and everyone was heading out to North Head, and it all moved so slowly that by the time we got there, they were heading up the hill and ready to jump off.

Like a film, you know, cutting-edge suspense.

The police moved super-fast then, crawling up the side of the hill like cockroaches, and one of them saying in this low voice, 'Take it easy. OK, guys. Take it easy.'

Celia and Saxon turned around with spotlights in their faces, dirty faces, small, frightened faces.

And Saxon just sat right down on the ground and burst into tears, like big sobbing tears. Celia was kind of half dragged down when he did that because their hands were held so tight, but she wrenched her hand away from his, and started running.

Then it got confused because police were shouting, 'Calm down now. We're not going to chase you', Celia's mother went pelting after Celia, and Saxon's parents were jogging up the hill to throw themselves at their sobbing little son.

Somehow Celia ended up jumping.

Just jumping, just flying.

Only she had run down the embankment so she was closer to the water. I don't even know what she was trying to do. I don't know whether she really meant to do this joint suicide with Saxon or even if she understood what it meant – like maybe she didn't realize that the fact you're doing it with your boyfriend doesn't make it different from killing yourself. And when she did jump, did she just throw herself off the edge because it seemed like the next obvious step in a movie?

Wait a minute. A very weird thing just happened.

Play that over again, Elizabeth.
  What did you just hear?
  'Don't cry, Christina. She'll be OK.'
  'Nick, don't touch the lady's flowers.'
  Play it again, Elizabeth.
  What did you just hear?
  'Don't cry, Christina. She'll be OK.'
  'Nick, don't touch the lady's flowers.'

With compliments,
The Instant Replay Society

Elizabeth,

Cut it out.
  Stop eavesdropping and imagining.
  Stop thinking of Christina.
  Stop writing to Christina.
  Stop it.
  This is Celia beside you. Don't you see her?

Best Friends Club

Elizabeth,

OK, you want to hear it again?
  'Don't cry, Christina. She'll be OK.'
  'Nick, don't touch the lady's flowers.'

With compliments, etc.
The Instant Replay Society

MESSAGE FOR CHRISTINA KRATOVAC:
WARD E, 11th FLOOR.
Is this Christina Kratovac of Brookfield High?
  If not, I am very sorry, and please throw this note away.
  If it is, I'm sorry to disturb you. I heard people walk
along the corridor, talking, and it kind of sounded like
your family, and I asked a nurse if there were any
Kratovacs around, and she said yes, someone just came
in, and they're in Ward E, 11th floor.
  I've been trying to decide for over an hour if I should
disturb you.
  I just want to make sure you're OK.
  I don't know if a nurse will deliver this to you or not.
I'm in Ward D, 7th floor.

                                         Elizabeth

Elizabeth,

Jesus. I can't believe you're here. Why are you here?
Are you sick? Oh God, everything's awful. Are you OK?
  I'm terrified.

It's my sister, Renee. Her appendix burst. They say it's 'touch and go'.

It can't be true.

I'm going to get my brother Nick to bring this to you. He'll wait if you want to write back.

I want to make sure you're OK too.

Love,
Christina

Christina,

God, you poor thing.

She'll be OK. I'm sure she'll be OK.

I'm OK. Don't worry about me. I'm here because Celia tried to. I'm sorry, I can't write that. She jumped off a cliff.

She's OK. She's not hurt. Just feverish. She was already sick, see.

She'll be OK.

Are you OK?

Elizabeth

No. Not really.

Jesus, Elizabeth, it's my fault.

It's my fault.

I was babysitting. Renee said she felt sick. I put her to bed with an ice cream container to throw up in.

What was I thinking?

Christina

Christina,

It's not your fault. Stop it.

That's what you're supposed to do when a kid feels sick.

Are your family there? What are you doing, just waiting? Is she conscious?

(Should I stop writing? Does your brother mind running the messages? He says he doesn't, but does he?)

Elizabeth

Please don't stop writing. It's keeping me alive.

Everybody's here except my grandfather, he's staying at home with Robbo and the baby. But aunts and cousins and Mum and Dad and everyone. We're in a waiting room. She's in intensive care, she's unconscious.

Oh Jesus, I can't write.

Everyone's here and nobody's crying. We're too scared to cry. Nobody's talking. My pen on this paper is the noisiest thing around.

My mother looks like her cheeks are dragging her mouth half-open. She's completely white.

Christina,

Your poor family.

I wish I could say something to make it all right.

My mum just told me that her cousin's little boy had a burst appendix a couple of years ago and he was fine.

My dad just told me that this is one of the finest hospitals in the country, and they'll be doing absolutely everything they can for your little sister.

Tell me if there's anything I can do for you. And my mum and dad say the same.

Elizabeth

Elizabeth,

Sorry for taking so long.

I hope I didn't frighten you.

Doctors came and talked to us.

Then we all cried, every one of us.

I think it's going to be OK. The doctors said that as she's made it this far, she's pretty sure to make it. Worst is through – that kind of thing.

She's sleeping now.

I think it's going to be OK.

God, it's hard to write when you're crying your eyes out, isn't it.

Most of my family are going home now, except my mum and dad and me. I couldn't stand to go home. I want to stay here all night and make sure.

Nick will take our last messages, then he's going home too. So we have to say goodbye.

I'm really sorry about Celia. I can't get my head around that yet. But it must be horrible for you. I hope she's OK.

Thanks for being here.

Christina

Christina,

Fantastic. I'm so glad.

Do you want me to come see you and sit with you for a while? I know it's a weird time for us to actually meet each other, but maybe it's a good time too?

If you prefer to just be with family, I understand.

Elizabeth

But I guess you have to be sitting with Celia?

Christina

Not really. I want to be here when she wakes up, but she won't until morning probably. She's OK. And she's got her mum and brother here, and my mum and dad, and Saxon's here too.

We could meet in the rec room that's on this floor. Just beside the lift. It's got a coffee machine and magazines and stuff.

I'll be the one in a grey T-shirt and jeans.

Would you like to?

OK.
Yes please.
I would.

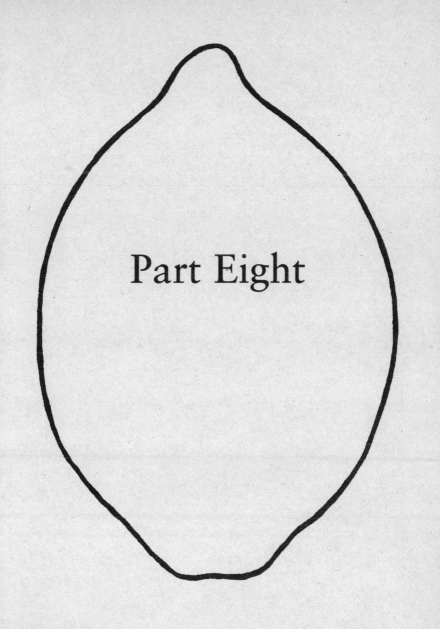

Part Eight

Dear Elizabeth,

It seemed incredibly weird to talk to you in person.
And now it seems bizarre to write to you too. But we
should keep doing it, shouldn't we? I'd really miss your
letters otherwise.

WELL.

Now I've got stage fright. Weird.

Jesus, though, it was so good meeting you. I felt really
nervous at first. I was worried we wouldn't have
anything to say, and I was terrified you'd take one look
at me and go: 'Uh, big mistake. Forget about getting
another letter from me until the sky starts raining
rhinoceroses.' You'd think my head would have been
filled up with worrying about my little sister, but it
generously made space for me to be terrified about
meeting you.

But then you were SO nice and friendly and funny. I
mean, you should be a social worker or a diplomat or
something – the way you kept the conversation going,
and asked all the right questions, and got me talking
about Renee and then about the rest of my family and
Mum's florist shop and everything. It was amazing. You
even had me laughing, which earlier that night I
thought I'd never do again.

The best thing of all is that you're exactly like your
letters. That's such a relief.

And you're not like a nice private school girl at all.

211

AND you stayed up all night talking with me. You must be a real party girl.

I'm putting a packet of marigold seeds in this letter, which you should plant somewhere sunny in your backyard. This is a good time to plant them. You don't have to worry about them, just kind of scatter them around in some dirt, and they'll figure a way to grow.

They're to say thank you. Seriously, you got me through that night. If you hadn't been there, well, I don't know what.

Renee's practically completely recovered now. She's still in hospital and she's kind of pale, and her eyes look spookily huge. But they say she'll be fine. And she's already starting to be her angelic self again, worrying that Mum looks tired, and making all the nurses adore her. They keep bringing out secret supplies of maple syrup to pour on her ice cream.

Talking about maple syrup, did I ever mention that my cousin Maddie's new boyfriend is Canadian? Maple syrup's like Canadian, isn't it? And so's your dad. Or does he just live in Canada? Wow, I should have figured that out by now. Sorry. Anyway, I've now met the Love-of-Maddie's-Life because my entire extended family have moved into our house to help us cope with the Renee Crisis.

It's nice of them all to be so supportive, but what it actually means is that Mum and I spend our lives doing washing-up, laundry, cooking and cleaning. Plus the family bring their own mini-crises with them, like bonus crises – everyone wanting to floss their teeth and pump up their air mattress at the same time each night, and everyone wanting brekky at a different time each morning.

212

Mum and I went to the supermarket and bought one of those giant packs filled with lots of little breakfast cereal packages – you know, Fruit Loops and Special K and Coco Pops – so everyone could have their favourite. It turned out that everyone's favourite is Coco Pops.

Maddie's parents are staying too, which is why I got to meet Maddie's boyfriend. She came over on the weekend, and brought him along. (Maddie doesn't seem capable of spending more than 24 hours without him.) That complicated sleeping arrangements on Saturday night even more, because we had to make sure Maddie and the boyfriend were the greatest possible distance away from each other within the confines of our house. Otherwise some mysterious magnetic force might have sent them crawling over sleeping grandparents and aunties to get it on together underneath the piano stool.

The Boyfriend seemed OK. He liked hanging out with the kids more than the grown-ups, and the kids all adored him. So the grown-ups ended up adoring him too, because he kept the kids occupied playing soccer or going on make-believe jungle expeditions. I'm reserving judgement on whether I adore him or not. He seems kind of jittery to me, kind of unreliable – like at any moment he's going to take off, and Maddie's going to follow, and there'll be a whole new Maddie-running-away-with-her-boyfriend scandal.

School's like this inconvenience at the moment, taking up too much of the time that I should be spending taking care of family crises. Still, it's also a relief to be away from all the chaos; like a holiday. And if it wasn't for History classes I wouldn't be able to write to you, would I?

Derek and I had a really nice conversation at lunch time today. He was upset about Renee – he told me he misses my whole family, then he said, 'All of you, I mean, I miss all of you.'

So, but I've been talking about myself too much. How are you going now? I should have asked this earlier, but I wasn't sure whether you want to talk about it. Don't worry if you don't. But how are Celia and Saxon? I mean, emotionally. And how are you about that? I can't imagine how you must feel, it must be just overwhelming.

Are you still training? Your half marathon must be coming up really soon. I liked the way you talked about it at the hospital – I think I ALMOST started to understand why you do it. Not that you'll ever see me within 15k of a pair of running shoes.

Anyway, you've got my number now, so call me any time you want to. And maybe we should see a movie some time?

Love,
Christina

ELIZABETH!!! OVER HERE! ON THE TABLE! BY THE HYDRANGEA? IT'S A NOTE FROM YOUR MOTHER !!!

YOUR FATHER CALLED ABOUT NEXT WEEKEND. BUT DON'T FORGET YOU AND I ALREADY TALKED ABOUT A WEEKEND ON THE COAST, JUST YOU AND I.
  I'VE DISCOVERED A CAMP CALLED 'SHORT

RETREATS FROM THE RIOTS OF YOUR LIFE' AND I'M
TAKING THE BROCHURES OVER TO CELIA'S MUM. I
THINK SHE NEEDS SOME PROFESSIONAL HELP, OR AT
LEAST A SHORT RETREAT FROM THE RIOTS OF HER
LIFE.

CELIA'S HOME FROM THE HOSPITAL AND WANTS TO
SEE YOU - COME ON OVER AND JOIN US WHEN YOU
GET IN.

LOVE,
MUM

P.S. JUST BEFORE YOU COME, HOW ABOUT WATERING
THIS HYDRANGEA AND THE FIG TREE IN THE
SUNROOM?

Dear Elizabeth,

Having trouble sorting out what matters most? Having trouble
scheduling quality time with an emotionally dependent mother,
bearable time with an eager-to-make-up-for-fifteen-years-of-
absence father, training for the Forest Hill Half Marathon,
replying to the letter of a new friend, visiting an old friend who
has just attempted suicide, and watering house plants?

Not to mention, of course, the inconsequential matter of
homework?

Perhaps we could interest you in an Introductory Package Deal:
two weeks at our exclusive mountain retreat undertaking our
rigorous, vigorous training course! Each day you will learn a new
strategy for managing your time! Learn to select your favourite
family member! Learn to TRICK people into thinking that you're

215

spending time with them, when in fact you're home doing your Maths assignment! Do they really need YOU in the same room as them? Perhaps a hologram of you would do fine!

Fill in the application form below and send it back to us quick smart!

Keep smiling!
Priorities Come First! Pty Limited

P.S. Tick this box for even more junk mail!

Dear Ms Elizabeth Clarry,

Actually, why not come to our camp?

We are confident that we can interest you in our BEDS.

We offer waterbeds, four-poster beds, camp beds, beds of nails and flower beds!

We are equally confident that we can entice you with our PILLOWS.

We offer fat pillows, skinny pillows, boomerang pillows, vibrating pillows, satin pillows, silk pillows, Santa Claus and Snow White pillows!

Here at our camp you can snuggle under feathery quilts and blankets, warm your toe-tops with hot-water bottles, and cuddle teddy bears. Listen to lullabies, draw the drapes on star-filled skies, yawn and click the off-button on your bedside lamp!

At our camp you can toss aside schedules, timetables, and worries. At our camp you need no clipboards and notepads!

At our camp all you do is climb into your bed and you sleep, sleep, sleep, sleep.

Call us.
The Land of Nod Inc.

216

Dear Christina,

Are you crazy? Of course we should keep writing. What would be the point in going to school if I couldn't check the cardboard box outside the upper staffroom for your letters?

There'd be no point. I'd have to stop going.

But I'd also like to go out or something again, because I really liked meeting you in person. Although I can't BELIEVE you were nervous about meeting me. I just can't believe it. I think you're making it up. Or you're getting yourself confused with me – think back, Christina – remember? *You* were the perfectly calm and graceful one, *I* was the one tripping over coffee tables and gabbling like a lunatic. You remember now?

Hey, and how come you never told me how pretty you are? Not that I assumed you were grotesquely hideous or anything, but I had no idea you looked like a supermodel. That was such a shock. No wonder I tripped over the coffee table.

I REALIZE you couldn't have said in a letter: 'Oh yeah, another thing about me. I'm a goddess. I should actually be making millions on the catwalk but I just have to study for my History exam first.' But STILL, you could have given me some kind of a hint, the tiniest warning.

I had actually started writing a letter to you at the hospital, before I realized you were also there. But I won't bother to finish it or send it to you. I was just ranting about Celia really; and I already did that that night.

And you were such a great listener. Especially since you had your own things to worry about. You shouldn't have sent me the marigold seeds 'cause it should be ME thanking you. But thank you very much for them. I've never grown anything before. I'm excited about becoming a gardener.

I'm so happy that Renee's getting better now. Celia seems OK too, although still a bit weird. Then again, Celia's always weird so it's hard to tell if this is a new weird or not.

She was actually OK physically the morning after I saw you, and she could have gone home, only they kept her and Saxon there for counselling. It's compulsory if you attempt suicide. It was awful really – Celia was saying things like, 'I didn't actually mean to go *through* with it, you know, so can't I go home now?' (Saxon's head kind of leapt backwards when she said that, as if he was in a car that suddenly braked.) But the hospital people just said, Sorry, no choice. They HAD to stay there, and get examined to make sure they didn't have any mental illnesses, like schizophrenia or manic depression or something.

In the end, the psychiatrists decided there were no pre-existing conditions, and that they were just highly-strung kids who had a slight case of inability-to-see-the-consequences-of-their-behaviour. Something like that. And they still have to go to counselling twice a week.

They're both taking some time off school, and lolling around at Celia's place together, which doesn't seem very emotionally invigorating to me. Saxon's always at Celia's even though his mother has FORBIDDEN him from seeing her any more – which has brought Celia's mother and my mother together in a united bond of hatred for Saxon's mother.

EXAMPLE—

Celia's mum: It's like pruning a rose bush with an axe! Can she not see that our children are in LOVE? Can she not see that the rose of love is a thorny one and that of COURSE there will be glitches as it heads its way to a glorious flower of togetherness?!

My mum: Once a fascist dictator always a fascist dictator. Why, I knew this sort of thing would happen way back when she was the driving force behind banning rollerblading in the shopping mall. Banning rollerblading! I know, I can't believe it either. Thin edge of the wedge is what this is, you mark my words.

Celia's mum: Freedom! The children must have freedom!

My mum: Thin edge of the wedge, I tell you. Mark my words.

I'm not sure what my mother means by 'thin edge of the wedge'. Does she think that someone who bans rollerblading will automatically ban her son from seeing his girlfriend, and that someone who bans her son from seeing his girlfriend will automatically take control over the country via a military coup and lock everyone up in their laundries?

But I do kind of like the way she hates Saxon's mum – especially as she secretly also seems to hate Saxon. She confessed it to me driving back from Celia's the other day. 'It's COMPLETELY the wrong thing to separate a young couple who are as smitten with each other as those two are,' she was ranting away. Then, just before we pulled in to our driveway: 'Still, it's beyond me what Celia actually SEES in that boy.'

It's strange how happy I was to hear that. But I have

to agree with her – I've been spending a lot of time over at Celia's trying to be a supportive friend – but it's impossible because he never stays more than a millimetre away from her, and he never stops gazing and moping at her. Actually, he reminds me of that dog you told me about that belongs to your next-door neighbour. He practically throws himself on the ground in front of Celia and begs her to scratch his tummy.

It's just not attractive.

I tried talking to Celia about her letter to me (difficult with Saxon the puppy-dog always around, but I got Celia on her own in the kitchen), and asked her if she wanted to talk about everything. She said maybe one day, but not right now and that she wasn't herself when she wrote that note and I should forget it. Then she climbed up on the kitchen table and did a trapeze jump through the living room door and onto the couch, nearly killing Saxon.

She's supposed to be taking it easy while she recovers but she's definitely getting her energy back.

My parents are being stupendously nice to me at the moment which is very weird. They were both at the hospital for most of the night when Celia was there – somehow Dad got phoned in the Celia crisis. He and Mum asked the doctors all the right questions, and were perfectly supportive and soothing with Celia's crazy mother and Saxon's outraged parents. We were actually like a FAMILY.

Although a weird sort of family – with the parents being eerily polite with each other. EXAMPLE:

Mum: So, Albert, how is your work with the airline?

Dad: It's going very well. And how is your work at the agency?

Mum: It's going very well. And how are your family?
Dad: They're very well. And how are your family?
Mum: They're very well. And (etc, etc, etc).

Mum was watching him VERY closely when she asked about his family, trying to get clues about the *affair* (she also asked questions like where was he living, oh, and what's that like, oh, and how big is your place, oh, and is that big enough for you, oh, I suppose if you're living on your *own* it must be, etc, etc, etc). But she got nothing out of him except for a classic performance of Mr Smooth and Polite.

Dad actually drove out here on Sunday afternoon and took me for a movie and a coffee just in Castle Hill, if you can believe it. Downmarket for him, huh? He was really nice about Celia, and somehow got me talking about the whole thing – about how Celia seemed to be changing, and about how I felt guilty about not being a supportive enough friend, but that deep down I was just tired of feeling sorry for her, especially since I rescued her from the evil circus and all she did to pay me back was steal the boy I liked.

I know, I can't believe I told him all that stuff. I think I partly did it because I was hoping to get something personal out of him too. Like: 'Well, all this is very interesting, Elizabeth. And it reminds me of my own personal crisis. I've been cheating on my wife, you see, living with another woman, what do you think about *that?*'

But all he said was that friendships go through fluxes and to hang in there and it would turn out for the best, he was sure. And then he asked me about the half marathon and said he thought I might be overdoing it, and too much running could wear me out. (He also said that he's heard you can stop tights running with a little clear nail polish, so maybe he should stop ME running with the same thing, ha ha ha. Why do ALL fathers have the WORST senses of humour in the world, please?)

Wait a minute.

SORRY. I just had to stop writing for a minute. I'm in English at the moment and I was writing along happily with Mr Botherit's voice like a kind of background music when suddenly the background music began to turn into eerily familiar words. It turned out he was reading out MY assignment to the class. You know we had to write a letter explaining why we shouldn't write an essay on *My Brilliant Career*? He gave mine the best mark. Ha. It was a dirty trick getting me to do it, and now he's pulled another one giving me the best mark. Now I feel like I HAVE to do the next assignment so I can get more praise. It's evil psychological game-playing and I'm going to resist it at all costs.

The bell's ringing and I'm going to miss my bus if I don't leave right NOW.

Love,
Elizabeth

Dear Elizabeth,

I know I told you I'd be out of the state by now and you should forget my existence. But you've probably already noticed that I'm still on your bus every day. All us Brookfield boys are still here.

I also promised that I wouldn't write to you again, but Christina told me today that she met you at the hospital when her little sister was sick. She told me how you stayed with her the entire night and she told me you were wonderful.

So I just had to write and say that you're a legend, you know that, don't you?

You're also incredibly beautiful.

The Stranger

Dear Elizabeth,

We regret to inform you that your application must be refused.

A 'crush' does not count unless it is directed at somebody specific. A 'crush' that is directed at three young men simultaneously, which will crystallize into a specific crush when a specific condition has been met; a crush which is entirely contingent upon which of three boys happens to be the author of a series of short, garbled and inconsequential anonymous notes, simply fails to meet our definition of a 'crush'.

You must try a little harder, Elizabeth. Along with the Association of Teenagers, we are just about ready to throw in the towel.

Yours,
Young Romance Association

Dear Elizabeth,

Well yes, we see your dilemma, but we don't think that we can help.

To tell you the truth, we can't figure it out and we don't think you're going to figure it out either.

It is perfectly possible that it is Grunge boy, Quiet boy or Feral boy. All of them are plausible.

You can sit there on that bus seat and turn around as many times as you want on the pretext of working out what vehicles happen to be following the bus today. You do that, Elizabeth. You can run through your measly collection of clues backwards and forwards and upside down if you want to. You can stare into the eyes of every single one of those boys and watch as every single one stares straight back.

But you're just not going to work it out.

Yours,
Society of Amateur Detectives

Elizabeth,

On second thoughts. WHAT just happened? WHAT did you just hear?

Keep trying, Elizabeth! We're rooting for you!

Society of Amateur Detectives

224

Elizabeth,

Yes, we can replay that for you, sure.

'You're a legend, you know that, don't you?'

No, we cannot isolate the person who said it. Yes, we agree that the words were just spoken by a boy who was heading past you up to the back of the bus. Yes, we also agree that this may be of vital importance, given that an anonymous person used exactly that phrase in a note to you this morning. Yes, we can confirm that a short conversation took place, as two boys headed down the aisle past your seat, as follows–

Boy 1: You can have my ticket to the sax concert if you want.

Boy 2: You're a legend, you know that, don't you?

But we are not, nor do we have any association with, the Society of Amateur Detectives, and we therefore have no interest whatsoever in which of the boys at the back of the bus spoke those words. We are, quite frankly, bored by your dilemma.

All we do is replay.

The Instant Replay Society

Elizabeth,

As we just explained, all that we do is replay. We can take a GUESS that the two vital voices proceeded to the far right of the back seat. They were, after all, the only spaces still free. We can also guess that the words were spoken by Quiet boy and Grunge boy. We can take that guess for you, Elizabeth, yes.

But we cannot process the information.

All we can do is replay.

Here. A complimentary replay:

225

You're a legend, you know that, don't you?
High speed if you like:
You're-a-legend-you-know-that-don't-you?
Even faster? Sure:
You'realegendyouknowthatdon'tyou?
In slow motion:

You're

a

legend,

you

know

that,

don't

you?

In reverse? Sure:
? – you – don't – , – that – know – you – , – legend – a –
You're

In black-and-white, in colour, in 3-D, if you like, however you like, Elizabeth, we can replay.

But we simply cannot tell you which PERSON spoke those words.

Understand?

Sure you do.

The Instant Replay Society

Dear Elizabeth,

OK, this isn't fun any more. Renee's home from hospital and the family won't leave. We've got house guests coming out of our ears. Turn on the tap for some water and a house guest lands in your glass. Open a packet of Smiths Crisps and a house guest climbs out of the bag along with a salt and vinegar crisp.

You know how I said before I had no space for thinking – I mean, specifically for thinking about Derek? Well now I need more because I have to make a decision fast and I've got even less space than before. For crying out loud, my bedroom's been taken over by great aunts and I'm sleeping on the kitchen floor.

The thing is that Derek basically told me today that he might be interested in Katrina Ecclehurst. She's the girl who's been twirling her ponytail in his face and calling him Dezza? I don't think Derek's ACTUALLY interested, but he's kind of reached the point where he thinks: why not? If he wants to move on, she's making it super easy for him – the way she's acting she might as well strip naked, lie on her back and say, 'Take me, baby, I'm yours.'

So today Derek comes by my desk in the Science lab, does casual conversation while he's spinning petri dishes together, and happens to mention, 'Katrina wants me to go out with her this weekend.'

So I say, 'Are you going to?'

Derek looks me right in the eye and says, 'Should I?'

Then Rattlesnake is behind us, telling Derek he has to go sit in his special-no-distracting-the-class position at the front and I say, 'I don't know.'

And Derek says (as Rattlesnake is herding him along like he's an escaped cow), 'You let me know, OK?'

So now I need time to make up my mind, and I have to make it up real fast.

I don't even have time to write to you. And I'd really like to spend some time with you; like hang out together for a while. And J**** wants to meet you. Oops. I just wrote his name. Wait while I scribble over it. Anyway, your mystery admirer wants me to set up a meeting with you if you're interested. He said he likes you too much to keep being nervous and imagine if you float out of the bus window like your fairy princess friend did. He said he had a dream last night that you were on the bus and you stood on the seat, put your head out the window and started flapping your arms like wings. Next thing his dream changed location and he was zooming down a high-way in a high speed car chase with a very cool acid jazz soundtrack playing, but in the back of his mind was this tragic thought: Elizabeth has flown off to the moon!

So he has to act fast before that happens.

Plus he said he's seriously going to die if he doesn't get to have a conversation with you soon.

I told him you probably never want to be in the same room as him because you were so mad about the Black Cap incident.

But are you interested?

Gotta go but I'll just look at your letter, and let me say right away that you've got to be kidding. I'm seriously NOT supermodel beautiful and I ought to know because I see myself in the mirror every day, and I have to struggle not to throw up. Your brain must have been mixed up.

I can't BELIEVE that English teacher of yours. Giving you the best marks in the class. Bastard. Positive reinforcement like that should be against school regulations. You'd better stop going to his classes.

I've got heaps more to say about Celia and Saxon (the loser – he's probably a reincarnated poodle; they're the most pathetic dogs) and your parents, but I HAVE to go, and we HAVE to get together. (Stop having coffees with your dad and have one with me?)

Love,
Christina

Dear Elizabeth,

So Mystery Boy wants to meet you.
    Nervous?
    We are.

The Young Romance Association

Dear Elizabeth,

We hear Mystery Boy is dying to meet you.
    Nervous?
    So are we.
    You think he'll keep on liking you when he speaks to you in person? You think he'll ever want to see you again when he knows what you look like close up, when he hears your mixed-up sentences, when he sees you trip over your own ankles?

Yours with very little hope,
Cold Hard Truth Association

And what if he wants to kiss you, Elizabeth? What will you do about that?

Sincerely,
The Association of Teenagers

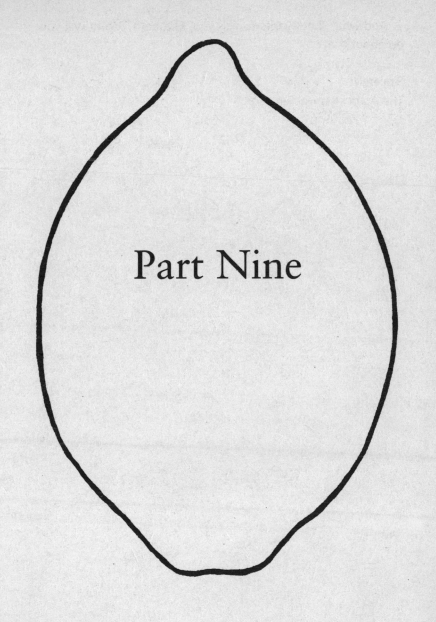

Part Nine

Dear Elizabeth,

OK, cue spooky music.

This is your 'brother' speaking, Elizabeth, and it's nice to meet you finally. But something seriously WEIRRRRD is going down around here.

Questions that spring straight to the cerebral cortex:

1. Why are you writing to me in Canada when I'm right here in Sydney?
   Possible answers:
   a. You think postal workers all over the world could do with a little challenging? Nothing like sending a letter across Sydney via the far northern hemisphere. That way it gets to spend six weeks in transit instead of one.
   b. You don't KNOW that I'm in Sydney right now.
2. In that case, WHY don't you know that I'm in Sydney right now?
   Possible answers:
   a. It slipped your mind.
   b. A certain unnamed *pater* chose not to tell you that he brought me and my mum along with him to Australia.
3. In that case, WHY did he choose not to tell you?
   Possible answers:

233

a. It slipped his mind.
b. I seriously have no clue.

There are a couple of other burning questions, but I don't think I should ask any more right now. I think we should chew them over out aloud, over a coffee maybe. What do you reckon?

The supernumerary weird thing is that I was staying with friends a couple of k's away from your home address last weekend. Spooky, no? So I kind of know the area, and which trains and buses I need to take to get there. Why don't I drop by some time and see you and work stuff out? I guess you know Dad's home number? Give us a call if you like.

Hope I get to meet ya.

Your brother,
Ricky

P.S. I get what you mean about trains, rocking you till you feel philosophical. Think about a 500 watt stereo next time you want to be truly rocked – and in the comfort of your own home. OK?

P.P.S. No, I don't think you're crazy for writing. I think it's extremely excellent.

ELIZABETH !!!

I'M SEEING A CLIENT BUT I'LL BE BACK FOR DINNER. PLEASE OCCUPY YOUR TIME UNTIL MY RETURN BY CONSIDERING THE MERITS OF SOCKS THAT ARE COVERED WITH TINY AUSTRALIAN FLAGS. WOULD YOU LIKE SUCH SOCKS? IF SO, WHY?

234

ANOTHER WAY YOU COULD OCCUPY YOUR TIME IS
CHOPPING ONIONS, PEPPERS AND MUSHROOMS, AND
CRUSHING GARLIC CLOVES, AND THAT WAY WE CAN
HAVE A RISOTTO FOR DINNER. HOORAY!

LOTS OF LOVE
FROM
YOUR
MUM

Mum,

I'm going for a run; back in time for dinner. Have
chopped etc. (Yes, hooray.) No thank you, I would not
like socks covered in Australian flags at all. Even if I was
barefoot in the Himalayas and my toes were about to
drop off from frostbite I wouldn't want them. Thanks
all the same.

About the risotto. Could we share it with someone?
Like a guest? What about if the guest happened to be
my stepbrother?

It turns out that Dad did bring his family along with
him to Australia after all – so the Other Woman we saw
at his place must be the Wife and not an Affair. And
now Ricky wants to come by and see us, and I've invited
him to dinner. OK? If you are seriously opposed I'll call
him and cancel. But aren't you dying to meet him? I
am.

Love,
Elizabeth

Dear Christina,

SERIOUS CRISIS in my family. OK, it's a minor crisis compared to your overload of house guests' crisis, and it's also minor compared to your choose-Derek-or-not-you-have-five-minutes-to-make-up-your-mind crisis. But still, it's unbeLIEVable.

And all caused by me.

Wait and I'll tell you what happened.

Ages ago I wrote a letter to my stepbrother in Canada for no real reason except that my dad was annoying me.

Yesterday I get a letter from my stepbrother saying he's right here in Sydney with his mum and my dad and he wants to come by.

Anyway, my mum and I were both, like, 'What is going on here? Why did Dad never mention that his son is in the country? Which one of us is he ashamed of? Does he not want us to meet the son because the son is a drug-dealing gangster? Does he not want the son to meet us because he thinks we'll bore him to death? And another thing, what if this risotto doesn't work out absolutely perfectly????'

(For some reason it was VERY important to Mum and me that we really impress this guy.)

So, a perfect stranger knocks on the door and we all stand in the front hallway and kiss each other's cheeks. He was about my age, and dressed like a normal person, not like a gangster, just in jeans and sneakers, so we were relieved about that. And he was polite, saying how he'd always wanted to meet us, and he hoped it was not an inconvenience, blah blah blah.

Then we all pretended nothing strange was going on and sat down to eat the best risotto ever created by human beings. And we talked about nothing really – just the differences between Toronto and Sydney and how ridiculously cold it is in Canada so WHY are people actually LIVING there, ha ha ha.

And then suddenly, while Mum was reaching into the cupboard to get some tinned peaches for dessert, the Guest of Honour said: 'So. You didn't know that my mother and I were in Double Bay with Dad?'

We said no we didn't know, and that Dad had said he was leaving his family in Canada.

'Dad told *us* we could never meet because you guys hated us,' he said.

Then all three of us spent some time over peaches and ice cream, making up crazy reasons why Dad might want to keep us apart. You know, anxiety that we would get together and talk about how awful his toenails are. That kind of thing.

Then my stepbrother looked at me and said, 'Weird, isn't it? That we've never met? Seeing as we were both created by the same guy?'

For a moment I thought he meant God or something, but then I decided he was not the religious type and he was actually talking about my father.

I said, 'Well, not really.'

Mum said, 'Well, not exactly.'

He said, 'Albert Clarry is your father, isn't he? And he's my father too – so . . .'

And Mum said gently, 'Is that what they told you? Oh dear.'

And Mum and I were like, 'Oh gosh, how awful' to each other, and this guy's sitting there going, 'Uh, I don't think there's any mistake. I think I know who my father is.'

And then Mum suddenly climbs onto her chair and shrieks, 'My God! The Clarry ears!'

And we both looked straight at his ears.

And she was right. He has exactly the same ears as me, and I have exactly the same ears as my father.

'How OLD are you?' my mother demanded.

It turned out he's about three months *younger* than me.

He was really embarrassed, apologizing, saying he didn't realize that we didn't know, and trying to cover his ears with his hair.

'Well, how about that?' my mother said, very calm and friendly. 'Albert was getting somebody else pregnant right around the time I found out I was pregnant. What do you know?'

Then my BROTHER apologized again and said he should probably call a cab and go home.

So that's the story.

My father's family has been here the whole time, and he could never let us meet because he had this wicked secret. He didn't meet someone with a kid, fall in love and leave my mum and me. He met someone, got her pregnant, and left my mum and me.

And it turns out that I've got myself a half-brother.

Anyhow, after my brother left, my mother went slightly mad. She started tipping furniture upside down and cleaning out the laundry cupboard, and when I said, 'Mum, take it easy,' she burst into tears. Then she was calm for a moment and said it all happened fifteen years ago and she's completely over my father, so why would it bother her now, and she'll just have a glass of wine to calm down, and then she threw the glass of wine against the wall.

Next she phoned my father and had a private conversation. She came out practically shouting, 'That CHILD of a man. That weak-kneed, yellow-toenailed, pathetic, piddling, chicken-clucking COWARD of a man!'

Then she decided that she wasn't going to let a chicken-clucking, yellow-toenailed coward get to her, and that she was determined not to have a nervous breakdown. She made a few phone calls and next thing you knew she'd arranged to go on a Short Retreat from the Riots of Your Life. It's something she had set up for Celia's mother, but now she's taking her place. (Celia's mother was having doubts about it anyway because it didn't seem to have 'quite enough of a mystical component' for her. No magic crystals and no tarot card reading.)

So that's partly why I'm writing to you now. My mum is leaving tomorrow and she'll be gone for this weekend and she said I should have some friends over on Saturday night, and I think you should be one of the friends. She's worried I'll just spend the next 48 hours training since the half marathon is a week away and she thinks it's tragic for a teenager to spend a weekend jogging. So, why don't you come? We could have a video party or something, and I'll invite Celia and Saxon too, and you can bring your cousin Maddie and her boyfriend along.

I'm sending this right away so maybe you'll get a chance to reply before you go home today. PLEASE say you can come.

Love
from
Elizabeth

P.S. And if you want to, you can ask your friend to the party on Saturday night – the Anonymous Note-Writer boy from the bus. Anyway, he can come if he wants to. If you think it's a good idea. I'm too nervous to meet him on my own.

Dear Elizabeth,

I can't BELIEVE the story about your brother. Your life is full of amazing stories.

I'm writing fast to get this to you before you finish school today. I really want to come on Saturday night. FANTASTIC. I'll check with my mother because she might not like me leaving her with all the relatives. But I think it'll work out – less people sleeping in the house means more room for air mattresses. And Mum will be happy because of Maddie and her boyfriend coming along. They'll definitely want to come – Maddie's dying to meet you because I talk about you all the time.

And I just asked your mystery admirer if he wants to come (I hope you really meant that) and of COURSE he wants to. Who are you kidding?

I'll call you tonight. Or you call me. And we have to talk more about your brother/mother/father. Family scandal, huh?

Love,
Christina

Dear Elizabeth,

You have nothing in the world to be nervous about. Christina is wonderful and you both got on deliriously well at the hospital that night. You'll have a fantastic time. The party will be a stupendous success. Christina and Celia will get on fine, and Maddie and her boyfriend will be delightful new friends and just what you need.

The Stranger boy likes you and there's no reason why he should stop. Just calm down and look forward to it, Liz. That's a girl.

Sincerely,
The Take-a-Deep-Breath-and-Calm-Down Society

Dear Elizabeth,

In fact, you have EVERYTHING in the world to be nervous about.

You think Christina will like you after a Saturday night together? You think one night in a hospital, when you were both in crisis, can actually tell you anything about whether you'll get along?

You think you know how to have a PARTY on your own? What food do you get? What drinks do you get? What video do you get? When do you put the video on? Who's in charge of the remote control? What music will you play? Will people DANCE? Will people COME? Isn't seven people too FEW for a party, Elizabeth?

You haven't got a clue, have you?

And another thing: you think you can suavely meet a bunch

241

of strangers INCLUDING the boy who thinks he likes you (without ever having even spoken to you) and manage to KEEP him liking you?

Do you have some kind of a DEGREE in stupidity, girl? If not, we'd like to offer you an honorary one right now!

Yours,
The Association of Teenagers

Elizabeth,

Uh. We agree.

Yours etc,
Cold Hard Truth Association

To: ELIZABETH CLARRY
From: HER MUM
Re: WHY DO I HAVE TO FILL THIS FORM IN ANYWAY?
No. Pages:

DEAREST ELIZABETH,

HERE IS THE FAX THAT I PROMISED, TO LET YOU KNOW THAT I ARRIVED SAFELY AT 'SHORT RETREATS FROM THE RIOTS OF YOUR LIFE' AND FRIDAY AFTERNOON HAS PASSED WITHOUT ANYONE TRICKING ME INTO JOINING A RELIGIOUS CULT. HOW PECULIAR TO WRITE A FAX TO YOU! YOU'LL HAVE TO STICK IT TO THE FRIDGE WITH A MAGNET BEFORE YOU READ IT, OTHERWISE YOU WILL BE CONFUSED.

IT'S FABULOUS HERE AND I AM SURE THAT I WILL
RETURN TO THE RIOTS OF MY LIFE VERY SERENE.
YOU WILL NOT RECOGNIZE ME AND MAY HAVE TO
SHAKE ME TO GET THE CALM, BEMUSED EXPRESSION
OFF MY FACE.

INDOOR ACTIVITIES INCLUDE BUBBLY SPA BATHS,
MASSAGES, MANICURES AND 24-HOUR JIMMY
STEWART MOVIES, BECAUSE ALL OF THESE THINGS
ARE SOOTHING.

OUTDOOR ACTIVITIES INCLUDE MUCKING OUT HORSE
STABLES AND BOTTLE-FEEDING LAMBS BUT I HAVE
EXPLAINED THAT THESE THINGS SEEM QUITE RIOTOUS
TO ME, SO I HAVE A SPECIAL EXEMPTION.

IN BETWEEN ACTIVITIES WE HAVE GROUP
DISCUSSIONS AND WE ALL TELL THE STORIES OF THE
RIOTS OF OUR LIVES. EVERYONE WAS VERY EXCITED
BY THE STORY ABOUT YOUR FATHER AND RICKY-THE-
SECRET-SON BECAUSE IT WAS MORE SCANDALOUS
THAN MOST.

THE TEAM LEADER OFFERS EXPLANATIONS FOR
WHY THE RIOTS OF OUR LIFE ARE GETTING US DOWN.
IT TURNS OUT THAT THE REASON I REACTED BADLY
TO RICKY WAS THAT I HAVE SUBCONSCIOUS INCEST-
RELATED ANXIETIES AND I FOUND HIM DISTURBINGLY
ATTRACTIVE.

THIS IS RUBBISH OF COURSE, BUT VERY FUNNY AND
I NOW FEEL MUCH BETTER.

ONE VERY EXCELLENT THING ABOUT THIS PLACE IS
THAT THEY ARE GOING TO GIVE US CHOCOLATE AND
PORT EACH NIGHT OF THE WEEKEND, BECAUSE IT
TURNS OUT THAT CHOCOLATE AND PORT ARE VERY
INSIGHT-INSPIRING. I'M PLANNING TO HAVE LOTS OF

DRUNKEN INSIGHTS AS SOON AS I FINISH THIS FAX,
WHICH IS LOVELY. (ELIZABETH, YOU DON'T THINK I'VE
BEEN <u>NEGLECTING</u> YOU AS A MOTHER, DO YOU? I
JUST HAD AN INSIGHT THAT MY LACK OF INTEREST IN
BOTTLE-FEEDING LAMBS MIGHT SUGGEST THAT I AM
LETTING YOU DOWN. AM I?) YOU WOULD BE PROUD OF
ME BECAUSE I HAVE BEEN A PARTICULARLY <u>ACTIVE</u>
MEMBER OF THE GROUP. THIS AFTERNOON I STARTED
MY OWN REBEL DISCUSSION GROUP FOR PEOPLE WHO
DON'T FEEL LIKE DISCUSSING THE RIOTS OF THEIR
LIFE ANY MORE. IN MY GROUP, WE TALKED ABOUT
ISSUES LIKE KNEE-LENGTH SOCKS COVERED IN TINY
AUSTRALIAN FLAGS AND WHAT MIGHT BE GOOD
ABOUT THEM. BRAINSTORMING SEEMS TO BE VERY
GOOD THERAPY FOR THE WOMEN.

SEND ME A FAX BACK TO THE NUMBER ON THE
LETTER HEAD, AND TELL ME HOW YOUR PARTY GOES
ON SATURDAY. GOOD LUCK! AND GOOD LUCK WITH
THE ANONYMOUS BOY FROM THE BUS <u>IN PARTICULAR.</u>
(YOU ARE A VERY GOOD GIRL FOR TELLING ME
ABOUT THAT. IT IS THE KIND OF THING A GIRL
SHOULD TELL HER MOTHER.) I'M SURE HE WILL
<u>ADORE</u> YOU BECAUSE YOU ARE <u>BEAUTIFUL</u>, AND I AM
<u>DYING</u> TO FIND OUT WHICH ONE IT IS. OK?

LOTS AND LOTS OF LOVE
YOUR
MUM

To: Mrs Clarry, c/o Short Retreats from the Riots of
Your Life
From: Elizabeth Clarry
Re: You should always complete forms, Mum
No. Pages: 5

Dear Mum,

It turns out that I'm a FABULOUS cook and Christina
asked why and I had to say it was because of you. You
neglected me so much that I had to learn to fend for
myself. So next time you have an insight about being a
neglectful mother, have another insight that in FACT
neglect has been very useful for me.

Anyway, it was very nice of you to take a break from
massages and manicures to write to your neglected
daughter. So you can't be that bad.

How does the camp leader feel about your rebel
discussion groups? And do the women know that you're
using their ideas for your advertising copy? Because I
think there might be some professional/ethical issues
to deal with, no?

I had the party last night and it was fantastic. I mean
a proper party success. I made genuine *hors d'oeuvres*
because I found recipes in your book (you meant me to
use the housekeeping money for smoked salmon and
caviar, didn't you?), and we all drank some of your
Bacardi with Coke, then we danced, and then we
watched three horror movies. And everyone slept in
the living room in sleeping bags and told ghost stories.

The Anonymous boy came and I'm not going to tell
you which one he was until you get back, and that will

be a way of making sure you actually come back. I'll just tell you this: he was very cool and especially talented at ghost stories. I think he might be a genius or something. He also knows magic tricks – and when he does them his fingers move as if they were flickering flames. He did some card tricks which had something to do with matchsticks and which were very very funny. I don't know why they were so funny. Maybe because we were pretty tired by then.

Celia and Saxon got on incredibly well with Maddie and her boyfriend. The four of them discovered this shared dream about one day going to New York and becoming world-famous. I think our shared dream about going to New York and drinking café lattes is a lot better and more sophisticated but I politely didn't tell them about that. They stayed up talking on the back verandah way after the rest of us had fallen asleep, making their New York plans. It's good to see Celia making constructive plans instead of crazy, dramatic, not-thinking-about-the-consequences decisions.

Now I have to tell you something extraordinary. Which I've put off this far but I don't have enough self-discipline to put off any longer.

The extraordinary thing has to do with the party, OK? And it has relevance to YOU. Maybe you want to discuss it in one of your therapy sessions?

Before I tell you the extraordinary thing, you should try and guess. I'll give you some clues.

1. Christina's cousin Maddie lives in Double Bay.
2. Maddie's boyfriend lives in Double Bay too.
3. The boyfriend is Canadian.
4. Dad lives in Double Bay.

OK, have you worked it out yet?

Guess who Maddie's boyfriend is?

I bet you guessed it, because you're a very smart mum.

It's Ricky Clarry, my HALF-BROTHER.

Amazing, no? I know. It was very weird seeing him walk up the driveway, with this huge grin because he found it hysterical that it was the same place. We had a nice chat and I told him that we didn't hate him because we knew it wasn't his fault. He said all his life he had suspected that Dad was a bit of a putz, but he hadn't known how much of a putz, but still, if it wasn't for Dad being a putz, he wouldn't exist, so he wasn't sure how he should feel, exactly. I told him not to stress, so he said he wouldn't, so it was all OK.

I was kind of glad that Maddie's boyfriend turned out to be Ricky instead of another stranger because I was a bit scared about all the strangers. Although it was very weird to have him in the house and to keep thinking every now and then: My god, he's actually a *brother* or something.

Anyway, I hope it's not wrong of me to bring this up now – like you're supposed to be retreating from the riots of life and here I am bringing them straight back to you. Not that I think your Team Leader's very good at dealing with your Life Riots. Ricky's cute but I don't think that you're subconsciously attracted to him. One thing I was thinking is that it makes perfect sense for you to be upset. It was bad enough Dad leaving us for another woman after I was born; but to cheat on you while you were pregnant. I can't really think of anything lower than that. And then to lie about it to

247

you, and to lie about your reaction to his family for all these years. It's like he's never stopped cheating on you.

I hope you don't mind me saying that. It's just something I was thinking about, and I wanted you to know that I'm behind you. Let's just say that if I had to choose between my mother and my father, I'd choose my mother like a shot. OK?

Keep having fun at the camp and don't take any notice of your neglectful mother insights or your Team Leader's insights. Because they're way wrong. And don't worry, we didn't wreck the house last night. They're all still here fast asleep except Anonymous Boy – he left in a taxi really early this morning before I'd woken up – and I just got up because I wanted to write to you, but I'm about to leave and go running, so they might wreck the house while I'm gone.

Sorry about that.

See ya.

Love from your
daughter
Elizabeth

P.S. I just realized that I told you we drank your Bacardi. Do you want me to cross that bit out? Because you're not supposed to tell your mother that you raided her alcohol cupboard, are you? Everyone was saying I should refill the bottle with water so you wouldn't know, but I told them you'd be cool about it. Which is true, right?

To: ELIZABETH CLARRY
From: HER MUM
Re: ELIZABETH! YOU ARE WRONG! YOU MUST <u>NEVER</u>
FILL IN FORMS! THAT WOULD MAKE YOU A
<u>CONFORMIST</u>!
No. Pages:

ELIZABETH !!!

I AM FAXING YOU BACK RIGHT AWAY TO SAY THANK
YOU VERY MUCH FOR YOUR FAX WHICH WAS
DELIVERED TO ME WITH MY BREAKFAST CROISSANTS.
IT WAS NICE OF YOU TO WRITE, BUT IT WAS
EXTREMELY CRUEL OF YOU NOT TO TELL ME WHICH
BOY TURNED OUT TO BE ANONYMOUS BOY. YOU
KNOW THAT I DO NOT LIKE SUSPENSE. FOR EXAMPLE,
I ALWAYS READ THE LAST PAGE OF A DETECTIVE
NOVEL BEFORE I BEGIN READING IT, AND THEN DON'T
EVEN READ THE NOVEL ITSELF. YOU KNOW THAT
PERFECTLY WELL.
   BUT YOUR OTHER NEWS WAS <u>EXTRAORDINARY</u>. I
THINK IT'S PROBABLY A VERY MEANINGFUL
COINCIDENCE THAT YOUR NEW FRIEND CHRISTINA
TURNED OUT TO BE CONNECTED TO RICKY CLARRY. IN
SOME STRANGE WAY IT MAKES ME FEEL BETTER
ABOUT THE WHOLE THING.
   THANK YOU FOR YOUR NICE WORDS ABOUT ALL
THAT TOO. I WOULD ALSO CHOOSE YOU BEFORE
YOUR FATHER, LIKE A SHOT, SO WE ARE WELL SUITED
FOR EACH OTHER.
   AND I CAN'T WAIT TO MEET YOUR NEW FRIENDS.
PLEASE TELL THEM NOT TO PUT WATER IN MY
BACARDI.

I HAVE TO GO BECAUSE WE HAVE A
BRAINSTORMING SESSION LINED UP.
SEE YOU SOON.

LOVE,
YOUR MUM

Dear Elizabeth,

Just writing to confirm with you that the Anonymous Note-Writer has now been identified. We understand that the boy in question actually attended a party at your house last night? That while there he told ghost stories and did magic tricks?

In order that we can close our file could you please confirm that the boy was, in fact, Jared Henderson, alias Grunge boy?

All the best,
Society of Amateur Detectives

Dear Elizabeth,

Actually, before we close the file, can we just say this?

We suspect that, last night, when you stood at your front door and watched a car pull up, watched a passenger door open, watched a boy emerge – we suspect that right until that very moment, you believed that it was Quiet boy.

Intuitively, without any particular evidence, that's what you thought, isn't it?

And you were surprised, weren't you, to see that it was a tall boy, a lanky boy, whose knees came out of the car first and surprised you with their frayed black jeans? You were surprised to see the dark hair and the lean as he waved goodbye to his mother, and stood back from the car, and looked up at you with a wicked grin on his face?

One clue that might have given it away is this: Anonymous Boy must have had quick and magical fingers to get those notes into your bag without you noticing; Grunge boy must have had quick and magical fingers to slip his bus pass to his friend, that day. Remember, Elizabeth?

· You disappoint us!

Nevertheless, it was a pleasure working with you, and we wish you all the best in future unsolved mysteries, and we are,

Yours truly,
Society of Amateur Detectives

Elizabeth,

Grunge boy is sexier than Quiet boy.

His clothes are sexily scruffy, his hair falls sexily into his eyes, his eyes are sexily dark.

He can play the drums, he is a poet, and he is a magician.

You may have been surprised that it was Grunge boy, Elizabeth, but secretly – you're over the moon.

Aren't you?

The Young Romance Society

Dear Elizabeth,

We're all about to leave. Sorry we can't wait for you to get back from your run (I guess that's where you are and I bet I'm right, because I know you better than anyone else). We tried to clean up a bit but we couldn't get the salsa out of the carpet. I think Celia might have broken the vacuum cleaner too, and Ricky made it worse when he tried to fix it.

Everyone says they had the BEST time (and isn't it WEIRD about Ricky being your BROTHER?) but I had an even better time.

I'm going to call Derek when I get home. I'll tell him that I don't want him to go out with Katrina Ecclehurst. Actually, I'll tell him that if he goes anywhere near Katrina Ecclehurst I'll break his face. (Lucky he gave me extra time to let him know the answer on that one.)

And then I'll ask if he wants to help out with some flower arranging at Mum's shop this afternoon.

Thanks for all your smart advice about that last night, and for finally helping me make a decision. Call me later today if you want.

Love,
Christina

Dear Elizabeth,

Very well. The party was a success – there was dancing and drinking and you stayed up until dawn. Well done.

And you liked him a lot, didn't you? Grunge boy – or Jared. But you were just TOO nervous to talk to him, weren't you? You only talked to the whole group or to other members of the group. You couldn't look him in the eye even when you HAD to talk to him, like to offer him chips and salsa, or to ask him to pass the remote control.

Perhaps he was too nervous to speak to you directly too – or perhaps he just did not like you – either way neither of you said more than three words to one another the entire night.

And either way you're NEVER going to hear from him again. You know that, don't you?

Excellent.

Yours sincerely,
The Association of Teenagers

Dear Elizabeth,

All right. We take that back.

The telephone just rang and we understand it was Jared phoning to ask you out tonight. And it's only the day after the party too, which is actually quite remarkable.

You were perfectly friendly when you accepted (maybe too friendly?) and you didn't sound ridiculously nervous.

We have doubts about how you'll cope on the actual date, of course, but we believe we will pass you over to the Young Romance Society to deal with this.

With best wishes,
The Association of Teenagers

Dear Elizabeth,

No, we're sorry but we can't help.

We're way too frightened. We can't help with what you should wear or how you should act or ANYTHING.

You should try asking Christina.

Yours with regret,
The Young Romance Society

P.S. But let us know how it goes, won't you?

Dear Christina,

I'll send this when we get back to school, which will be too late to be any use, but I can't think of an alternative.

I'm completely confused. Jared just asked me out tonight. For a start, I'm confused because I thought he must HATE me by now. I mean, I didn't say a single word to him last night. And then he left early this morning so it was like proof: I messed up my chances.

Anyway, for whatever crazy reason, he must still like me – but if I was too scared to talk to him last night with other people around, I'll be a wreck tonight. He'll say one word and I'll collapse into a coma on the floor. And what should I wear? And what should I do with my hair? And what if—

Actually, wait a minute. This is ridiculous. I'm going to phone you.

Dear Elizabeth,

Well.

Welcome home.

Stand at the doorway and watch the car disappear down the drive; watch as its blinkers flash from the corner; listen as it turns and fades into the distance.

THAT was a success.

Look at yourself in the hallway mirror now – you DO look beautiful. The green in the earrings brings out the green in your eyes; the lipstick matches the crimson in your top.

Look at your hand as you clean your teeth, Elizabeth – look, you see that hand? You see how he held that hand, how he took that hand just as you left the cinema.

For three and a half minutes he held your hand. (After that, his mother was waving at you from the Exit door and drove you both home. But still.)

Close your eyes as you slip your nightie over your head, Elizabeth – remember how you talked right through the previews stopping just in time for the movie to start?

Remember how he apologized for all his anonymous notes, and how you made him promise never to apologize again, and how you made him smile by telling him you couldn't have survived without those notes.

And remember how you both admitted you were too nervous to speak to each other at the party, but you had a great time anyway, just knowing the other was there?

We think he's going to ask you out again.

In fact, we don't just think it. We're absolutely sure.

Sleep well.

Love,
The Young Romance Society

Dearest Elizabeth and Christina,

By the time you get this we will be in hiding. We are writing to you two because we love you, plus because we are so glad that you brought us together. Your party was fantastic – it was like a turning point for us. Because we discovered that we all have exactly the same goal. None of us can bear this monotonous suburban hell a moment longer and we have set out to fulfil that goal.

This is what our dream is – to go to New York and be EXPLOSIVE. To make ourselves FAMOUS. So we came up with the idea that we should parachute off the Empire State Building. (Maddie knows how to do it, Saxon has the money to buy parachutes, and Ricky knows someone who works at the Empire State Building who he says will help us avoid security.)

It might seem impossible but we have some unexpected ammunition up our sleeves and the fact is, we are going to do it. We have to be in hiding now to plan but as soon as we can manage it, we're flying to New York, and then we're really going to FLY.

Watch the American news on Saturday night, a fortnight from now. We'll be on it.

Love always,
Celia
on behalf of, and together with,
Celia and Saxon,
Maddie and Ricky

Dear Mum,

Sorry I'm not here to welcome you home. I'm doing a long run because the Forest Hill Half Marathon is next Saturday.

I hope you had a nice retreat from the riots of your life. Here's a new riot.

Celia and Saxon have run away again – and this time they've taken Maddie and Ricky with them.

Guess what else? They're planning to fly to New York and parachute off the Empire State Building.

We just had a Major Emergency Meeting at Christina's place – Celia's mother, Saxon's parents, Maddie's parents (Christina's Uncle Rosco and Auntie Belinda), Dad and his wife (I finally got to meet her – I'll tell you all about it later), Christina's parents, Christina's grandparents, Christina's great-grandparents, Christina's second-cousins – all sitting around Christina's living room eating coconut slice and drinking tea.

At first, most of the grown-ups thought it was ridiculous and of course they'd never get as far as the airport.

Then Celia's mother put her hand in the air and said, 'I'd like to make a contribution here.' Then she started to list all the extraordinary things Celia has done in her life.

Then Maddie's mother put HER hand in the air and said, 'Well, come to think of it, listen to some of the hijinks MADDIE'S got up to – you think becoming a trapeze artist is bad? Our Maddie has slid down drainpipes from a tenth-floor apartment and hitch-hiked to central Australia!'

After that everyone had their hand in the air, and everyone was talking at once. It became a kind of contest between parents, all wanting to prove how much more adventurous and dare-devil *their* kids were (and with Saxon's mother demanding the police or a lawyer because she blamed everything on Celia's mother and thinks she should be arrested).

Then Dad pointed out that Ricky knows New York quite well because they often go on family trips there from Canada.

Christina's great-grandmother said, well they might be young hoodlums but they'll never afford the cost of four airfares to New York.

Saxon's father said that actually Saxon has a tidy little inheritance which he can access whenever he wants.

Celia's mother said, 'If your son has paid for Celia to fly to New York, then you'd better keep an eye on that lawyer of yours because *I'm* retaining him to wipe you out.'

Dad said that Ricky *also* has quite a nifty amount of money in an off-shore account, and I had to put up my hand to say, excuse me but why don't *I* have quite a nifty amount of money in an off-shore account?

Then there was a lot of talk about whether they had passports, and where they might stay, and who exactly was going to let them up the Empire State Building with a parachute.

Christina and I thought we should just leave them alone and they'd come home in a week with their parachutes trailing between their legs.

But there was too much hysteria for that. The parents were determined that they should be stopped (even Celia's mother) and the only issue was how. So it was all arranged. For the next two weeks, everybody is going to help to try and find them. We're going to search the city and warn the airlines and guard the airports. And then, if we don't find them in time, Dad and Uncle Rosco (that's Maddie's father) are going to fly to New York and stake out the Empire State Building. Dad's already bought the tickets – he did his Big Man at the Airline thing, kind of coolly showing off about how he can get tickets for practically nothing. Uncle Rosco didn't seem that impressed.

See you soon.

Love,
Elizabeth

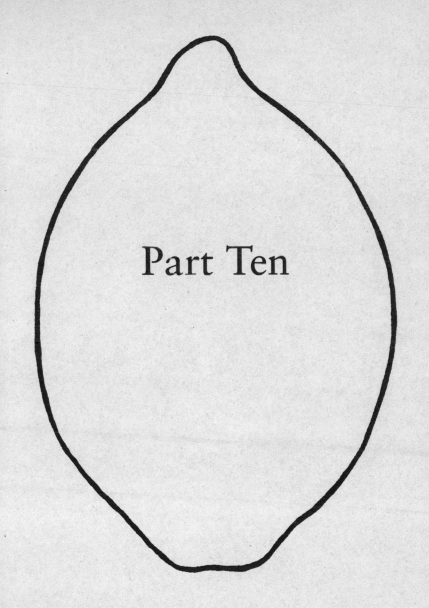

Part Ten

Elizabeth!

What are you doing RUNNING IN THE FOREST HILL HALF
MARATHON?

Run away! Run away from this madness! Escape these crowds
of runners!

Join the Search Party as they hunt alleyways and camping
grounds, scour airports, phone airlines, beg policemen to take
them seriously – help them track down Celia, and stop her
leading herself and her friends into disaster!

Stop this running nonsense! What on earth do you think you
are doing!!

With much concern,
Best Friends Club

Elizabeth,

Stay right where you are.

You've trained for this and you've trained hard.

Just take it steady; pace yourself; run slowly for now; there's
plenty of time for speed later. This is so easy you could do it
walking on your hands! You can't even feel the ground, really –
it's like you're a seagull that just caught a breeze.

Ignore all other messages, enjoy the rhythm of your pace, and
concentrate on your breathing.

Yours,
The Society of High School Runners

Dear Elizabeth,

OK, that's enough.
 Stop.
 I don't care whether you rescue Celia or not, I don't care
what you do. I just need for you to stop running. What you
actually have to do is lie down in a patch of shade somewhere.
See that bus seat? Sit on that. Go on. Take a seat.

Yours,
Cold Hard Truth Association

Dear Elizabeth,

Ignore everyone! Keep going! You can do this!
 You're SUPPOSED to be completely destroyed by running a
half marathon faster than you've ever run long distance before –
remember? This is a personal challenge!
 What do you mean 'no energy'? Of course you've got
energy! You've been carbo-loading for months! Look at the
people who have quit, Elizabeth! Look at them falling to the
side of the path, bending over, clutching their knees, lying flat
on their backs. THAT'S what it means to have no energy!

Yours with the best of luck,
The Society of High School Runners

P.S. Think about this. If Saxon was here as your running partner,
like he used to promise that he would be? By now you would
have politely asked if he minded you running on without him.
You were always better than him, Elizabeth. You'd have left him
eating your dust.

Dear Elizabeth,

It has suddenly occurred to us that maybe Celia is not your best friend any more?

I don't mean that she's not your FRIEND. She will always be your friend. You will always have a childhood full of memories between you.

But I wonder if you've drifted apart now and will never be quite so close again. And I wonder if it really, truly matters?

Just a thought.

Keep on running, baby.

Best Friends Club

P.S. Another thing – you see Christina on her bicycle, riding alongside, shouting at you not to quit? You think Celia would ever have done that?

P.P.S. Still, maybe you could tell Christina to put her camera away. A portrait of you with your hair flat with sweat, your cheeks bright red, and your face grimacing with the effort? The world just doesn't need it.

Dear Elizabeth,

Yes, we see how you might be distracted. We see how the thought of Jared's hands and wrists and forearms are difficult to eject from your mind.

But you'd better stop thinking about him, Elizabeth. It's slowing you right down.

Think about that woman up ahead instead – now why is a

woman wearing an overcoat and leg warmers so far ahead of
you, please? Go ahead. Overtake.

Kindest regards,
The Young Romance Society

Elizabeth,

I believe that the finish line is not so far now.
    I realize that your legs are so heavy they could drill straight
through this road. I realize that the only word to describe
how your lower back feels right now is 'agony', and that if
you stopped to think about it you might throw up on the
spot.
    But I think that, if you don't drop dead, you will make it to
that finish line.
    Still, perhaps dropping dead would be preferable?

Yours,
Sensible Suggestions at Your Service Inc.

Elizabeth! What are you doing?? There's something the matter
with you!! You're SPRINTING – you're SPRINTING towards the
finish line!! Have you lost your MIND???

Anxious but also Extremely Excited, Inc.

Elizabeth,

You finished.
   We're so proud of you.
   Now if everyone else would please shut up and let the poor girl have a break?

The Society of High School Runners

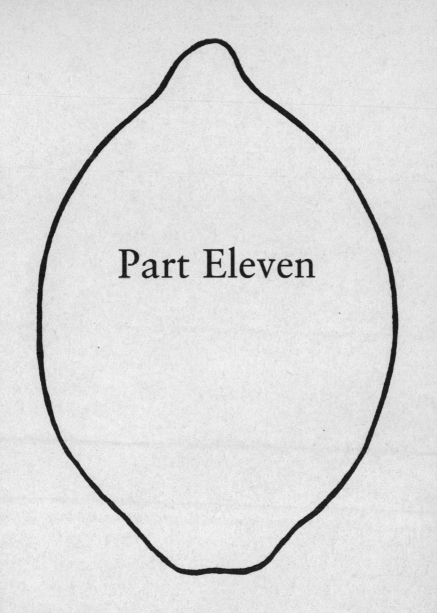

Part Eleven

ELIZABETH (AND CHRISTINA!) !!!!

WELCOME HOME.
 I DROVE HOME ALMOST AS FAST AS YOU SPRINTED
THE LAST BIT OF THE MARATHON, ELIZABETH. THAT
WAS <u>ASTONISHING</u>. CONGRATULATIONS !!! (ARE YOU
SURE IT'S NORMAL TO WALK HOME AFTER A
MARATHON?)
 GUESS WHERE I'VE GONE NOW?
 CELIA'S PLACE!
 GUESS WHY?
 YOUR MISSING FRIENDS ARE ALL THERE!
 THEY'VE BEEN FOUND !!!
 CELIA'S MOTHER PHONED ME, BUT SHE IS BEING
VERY MYSTERIOUS ABOUT THE DETAILS AND REFUSES
TO TELL ME UNTIL I GET THERE.
 CHRISTINA, YOU'D BETTER PHONE YOUR FAMILY
AND LET THEM KNOW THAT MADDIE IS ALIVE AND
WELL AND NOWHERE NEAR THE TOP OF AN
AMERICAN TOURIST ATTRACTION.
 ELIZABETH, YOU'D BETTER PHONE YOUR DAD AND
TELL HIM THAT HIS SON IS <u>STILL</u> IN THE COUNTRY.
 I'LL BE BACK AS SOON AS I HAVE THE DETAILS
AND WE'LL HAVE A CELEBRATORY CHOCOLATE CAKE
FOR THE BEST MARATHON RUNNER IN THE <u>WORLD</u>!!!

                              LOTS OF LOVE
                                  FROM
                                  MUM

271

P.S. I SUPPOSE SOMEONE HAD BETTER PHONE
SAXON'S MOTHER TOO. TRY TO AVOID BEING
UNNECESSARILY POLITE.

Mum,

I'm taking a shower if you're looking for me, and
Christina's just taken a bus home because she
wanted to tell her family in person. She'll be back
soon.

Thanks for phoning as soon as you got the details. I
can't believe that they have been living in the attic at
Celia's place all along.

I can't believe that they still had not agreed on the
best brand of parachute or worked out a way to get
plane tickets.

And I really can't believe that Celia's mother didn't
notice four extra people raiding her refrigerator while
she slept each night.

I phoned Dad and he didn't seem to care about
where they were. He's just happy that he doesn't have
to fly to New York with Uncle Rosco.

I phoned Saxon's parents too.

I would like to recommend that Celia's mother go
into hiding from Saxon's family lawyers. (Tell her to try
the attic.)

Thank you for the congratulations about the race. It
was just a half marathon, not a marathon, so it was a
piece of cake.

Still, one of my toenails has turned purple.

And I'm VERY excited about the chocolate cake.

Lots of love
from
Elizabeth

ELIZABETH !!! LOOK AT THIS NOTE !! SLIDING UNDER
YOUR BEDROOM DOOR!

I HAD A MARVELLOUS DAY. IT WAS EXCITING
WATCHING YOU AT THE MARATHON, AND EXCITING
WELCOMING YOUR RUNAWAY FRIENDS BACK FROM
THEIR ATTIC. IT WAS ALSO A LOT OF FUN
CELEBRATING WITH YOU AND CHRISTINA, WHO IS
LOVELY AND VERY FUNNY.
   I KNOW THAT IT IS THE MIDDLE OF THE NIGHT BUT I
JUST WOKE UP WITH A SUDDEN BRAINWAVE. I AM
GOING TO PUSH THIS NOTE UNDER YOUR DOOR, AND I
MIGHT KNOCK, BUT VERY LIGHTLY. YOU SHOULD ONLY
WAKE UP IF YOU REALLY FEEL LIKE WAKING UP.
   IT'S BECAUSE I HAVE AN IMPORTANT QUESTION TO
ASK YOU: IF DAD AND UNCLE ROSCO DON'T HAVE TO
GO TO NEW YORK AFTER ALL, WHAT'S GOING TO
HAPPEN TO THEIR PLANE TICKETS?

                                              MUM

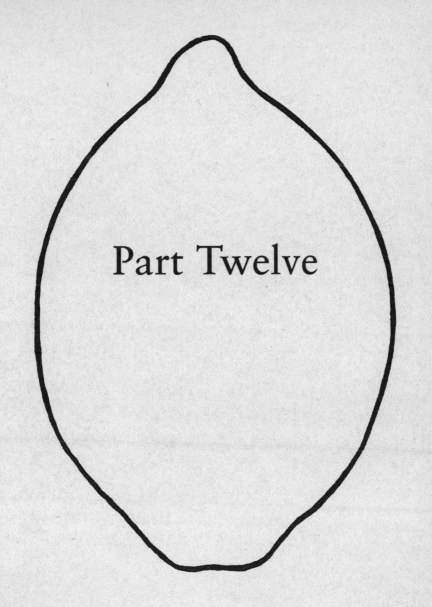

Part Twelve

Dear Elizabeth,

Yes, we realize that things are going quite well for you. We realize that you recently held a fantastic party, that you finished a half marathon in the TOP FIVE, and that you have just been asked out on another date.

But YOU realize, we assume, that NONE of this makes you into a teenager? You realize that you still fail to meet several of our regulations? You realize that Jared might have asked you out again, but you won't have a clue what to do if he wants to kiss you. You realize—

Dear Association of Teenagers,

I am writing to let you know that I chose not to finish reading your last letter. I am also writing to let you know that I am no longer especially interested in your opinions. In the last few months you have been very helpful pointing out my faults, tripping me over every time I was about to feel happy, and making me cry into my pillow each night before falling asleep.

I am very grateful for this but I would like you to remove my name from your mailing list. Before we end our correspondence, you should know this: last week I had a party with dancing, drinking and all-night talking.

Tomorrow I am going out AGAIN with the sexiest

guy alive, who I think is about to become my boyfriend. (OK, I don't know how to kiss him. But I have a feeling you're not supposed to TRAIN for kissing. I think you just do it. I think I can't wait for it to happen, actually.)

Next week, I'm going on a trip to New York City with my mum, to hang out in cafés and galleries, and check out the route of the New York Marathon.

And guess what else? I think I have a new best friend. So if you excuse me, I would like to go to sleep.

Write to me again? I won't even open the envelope. I'll rip it into tiny shreds and flush it down the toilet.

With very best wishes,
Elizabeth Clarry

A selected list of titles available from Macmillan and Pan Books

The prices shown below are correct at the time of going to press. However, Macmillan Publishers reserve the right to show new retail prices on covers which may differ from those previously advertised.

All Macmillan titles can be ordered at your local bookshop or are available by post from:

Book Service by Post
PO Box 29, Douglas, Isle of Man IM99 1BQ

Credit cards accepted. For details:
Telephone: 01624 675137
Fax: 01624 670923
E-mail: bookshop@enterprise.net